A tall, thin girl with blonde hair made what can only be described as an Entrance. Conversation ceased.

"Who is that?" someone whispered as the girl strode confidently up the aisle.

She paused midway. "Is this where tryouts for *The Taming of the Shrew* are being held?" She strode onto the stage. "I'm Angie Vogel," she said. "And I'm auditioning for Katharina."

She finished her audition to a roar of applause, entirely from the guys in the audience, I noticed, and floated down off the stage.

As she walked by with her nose in the air, she said, "Try to top that." I don't know how or why, but I was sure she was talking to me. Maybe it was because she was staring straight at me.

**Also by Marlene Perez**

Love in the Corner Pocket

Unexpected Development

Dead Is the New Black

Dead Is a State of Mind

Dead Is So Last Year

# The Comeback

BY MARLENE PEREZ

Point

Thanks to Amanda Maciel, super-editor, who made Sophie shine. And to Stephen Barbara, super-agent, and most of all, to my family, who are super-patient.



Library of Congress Cataloging-in-Publication Data

Perez, Marlene.
The comeback / by Marlene Perez.
p. cm.
Summary: High school junior Sophie can almost handle having her boyfriend and her lead in the school play stolen by a beautiful new student, but when her social status plummets, Sophie declares war.
ISBN-13: 978-0-545-08807-7 (alk. paper)
ISBN-10: 0-545-08807-0 (alk. paper)
[1. Popularity — Fiction. 2. Dating (Social customs) — Fiction. 3. Theater — Fiction. 4. High schools — Fiction. 5. Schools — Fiction.] I. Title.
PZ7.P4258Com 2009
[Fic] — dc22

2009000481



12 11 10 9 8 7 6 5 4 3 2 1 9 10 11 12 13 14/0

Printed in the U.S.A.
First printing, August 2009

*To the Mini-Ms.*

# Chapter 1

I hadn't asked to be popular. In the beginning, I hadn't even thought about it. The only thing I'd thought about was the cute boy with the brown eyes and floppy blond hair. He wasn't afraid to admit he liked chocolate chip cookies, Monty Python movies, and me. Only later did that boy turn into Connor, the most popular guy in the junior class. But when we were freshmen, he was just Connor, who loved cookies, and I was just Sophie, who thought she could love Connor.

We were happy. But then we became popular, and it happened so gradually that I hadn't noticed that, pretty soon, popularity was what our entire relationship was about.

Connor and I first met at the country club where our fathers played golf. My parents had just gotten a divorce and it was my dad's idea of father-daughter time to take me to the country club and then dump me at the pool while he hit the links.

So, I spent my days hanging out there with Monet. Back then, she'd just started calling herself that.

My best friend had interesting theories, one of which was that she had been given the wrong name. We'd agreed that since we'd both be starting high school in the fall, we would reinvent ourselves. To that end, I wasn't allowed to breathe a word of her real name to anybody.

Even back then, Monet and I had big plans. We were going to move to Los Angeles and become famous. She was going to rock the art world with her moody abstract paintings and I was going to become a film star. I was sure Monet was going to make it. She had the talent and drive to make it happen.

It was a little more complicated for me. You could look like a troll and be a character actor (in fact, sometimes troll looks were a plus), but a film star had to be beautiful. I was determined to have a physical metamorphosis and turn my plain old caterpillar self into a butterfly.

Back then, I'd just started to work out on a regular basis and was actually wearing a bikini to the pool for the first time. My braces were off and my hair was behaving. I remember thinking that I might actually be getting pretty. My transformation was well on its way.

Monet's older brother, Dev, was there, too. He splashed around the pool, showing off for a couple of girls in his sophomore class. They ignored him and so did we.

He hauled himself out of the pool to come bug us. "Imogene, can I borrow a dollar? I want something from the vending machine."

She ignored him.

"Imogene," Dev said.

"Don't you dare call me that in public," Monet hissed.

"It's your name," he pointed out.

"It's my *legal* name," she replied, "but I've told you, from now on I'm Monet, like the painter. And just for that, no, you *can't* borrow money."

Dev shrugged and dove cleanly into the water.

"He's a good swimmer," I commented.

Monet said, "He made the varsity swim team and it's totally gone to his head."

"He's on the *varsity* swim team?"

I made conversation, but I wasn't really paying attention. I was busy looking for someone. I'd had my eye on a gorgeous blond guy, Connor, who was on the swim team, too. We'd joked and flirted, but he hadn't asked me out yet.

"Well, it's the *only* swim team at Kennedy," Monet replied. Kennedy High School was an arts magnet school, mostly known for its drama and music departments.

We giggled. I finally saw Connor as he entered the pool area, and my heart sped up. Would he come over and talk to me? We'd met formally a few weeks before. Some loser guy had hassled me in the parking lot and Connor had gotten rid of him for me. But we'd been noticing each other since the beginning of that summer.

He took a seat next to his friend Chase. There were a couple of girls nearby, but Connor didn't pay any attention to them.

I kept my eyes on him, willing him to look up and acknowledge my presence, but he was absorbed in his conversation.

A few minutes later, Dev came out of the water and flopped down beside me.

"Dev, you're dripping water all over," I scolded, but I didn't take my eyes off Connor.

Dev followed my gaze and snickered. "You like that poser?" he said.

"I don't know who you're talking about," I said.

"Connor Davis," he replied. "That's who."

I flinched when I saw Connor raise his head and stare over at us. He'd heard us talking about him.

"Could you keep it down, Dev?" Monet said. She turned to me. "He is perfect for you. Cute but shallow."

"Hey, wait a minute!" I said.

"You know what I mean," she replied. "I'm not saying *you're* shallow, but Connor has future prom king written all over him. Mark my words, he'll be one of the popular kids at school." She said the word *popular* the way other people might say *serial killer.*

I noticed Dev was listening to every word and gave Monet a nudge to shut her up.

"Hey, watch this!" Dev did a cannonball into the pool, soaking us in the process.

"Dev, you idiot!" I said. My hair was drenched. I was at the pool to be seen, not to actually get wet. Connor was walking toward us with his best friend, Chase, and a girl I didn't know. The frizzies were imminent.

"What am I going to do?" I wailed to Monet. "I'm going to have clown hair in about ten seconds."

She surveyed me. "You look good, Sophie. Great, actually."

"But my hair!" I said.

"I think it looks fine," she said, "but if it bugs you, why don't you braid it?"

Genius. "Great idea," I said. I rummaged through my beach bag and found a couple of rubber bands and quickly did my hair.

"How are you two gorgeous women doing today?" Connor said.

Monet stifled a snort and then said, "I'm going to swim laps. Later." She got up and dove into the pool.

"This is Vanessa," he said. Who was she? His girlfriend? Was this his way of letting me down easy?

Vanessa acknowledged me with a wave and said something to Chase. She examined her nail polish, clearly already bored with me.

"Do you want to get together and hang out tomorrow night?" Connor said.

"You mean with you?"

He smiled at me. "I mean *me*, with *you*."

"I'd love to," I replied. "And maybe we can double with Chase and Tamara."

Chase shook his head frantically.

Vanessa's head snapped up. "Who is Tamara?" she said, suddenly interested in the conversation.

"She's Chase's girlfriend," I replied.

Vanessa shot Chase a look of pure fury and it dawned on me that perhaps I'd missed something.

"That's very interesting," she said.

"Take it easy, Vanessa," Connor said easily. "Tamara is my cousin. She and Chase are practically brother and sister. Sophie just saw him giving her a hug, right, Sophie?"

I wanted Connor's friends to like me. "R-right," I said. I left out the part about Chase's hand on her ass.

Vanessa melted and launched herself at Chase. "Oh, baby, I'm so sorry I doubted you."

"So we could go out with *Vanessa* and Chase," Connor continued.

I smiled at Connor gratefully. He'd rescued me from myself. I didn't even notice, at least not then, that he'd lied with the smoothness that comes with years of practice. Maybe I didn't want to notice.

During that summer, we became inseparable, and my blissful ignorance continued until our junior year. When everything fell apart.

# Chapter 2

The first day of my junior year was supposed to be a fabulous new beginning. Mr. Fanelli, the drama teacher, always held auditions the first week of school, but this year, auditions were after school on the very first day, which threw me off a little. Our high school drama department was putting on a production of *The Taming of the Shrew* and I was supposed to play Katharina to my boyfriend Connor's Petruchio. We were the It couple at Kennedy High and we were supposed to have starring roles to match.

I was certain I was going to get the lead. The only other serious contender, a senior named Alicia Grant, was modeling in Paris, which left the field wide open for me.

I hurried to Connor's locker. "C'mon, we're going to be late for the auditions." He was a sure thing, too. He wasn't a great actor, but he remembered his lines and always said them with enthusiasm. Plus, Fanelli was no fool. He knew that everyone at Kennedy would buy tickets just to see my gorgeous boyfriend onstage.

As Monet had predicted that summer day at the pool, Connor was, indeed, prom king material. And that's what I loved about him, because I had every intention of being prom queen. But before that, I needed to ace the audition.

"What's your hurry, babe?" he said.

"My hurry is that I want that part, Connor," I said. "And you're going to help me get it. Now move!"

"Okay, okay," he said. "Don't have a coronary."

He walked to the auditorium at a snail's pace. I would have walked ahead of him, but I wanted to walk in on his arm.

We opened the door and were surrounded by a group of sophomores. I smiled at them regally before I shooed them away. Then Connor went over to talk to some of his buddies and I slid into an aisle seat next to Monet. She was the stage manager for this production.

A minute later, a tall, thin girl with blonde hair made what can only be described as an Entrance. Conversation ceased.

"Who is that?" someone whispered as the girl strode confidently up the aisle.

She paused midway. "Is this where tryouts for *The Taming of the Shrew* are being held?"

She stood close to where I was sitting so I got a good look at her. Flawless skin, perfect figure, fake eyelashes. I hated her on sight.

To top it off, she was dressed in a very expensive pseudomedieval dress.

"She looks like she just came back from the Renaissance Fair," I muttered to Monet, but secretly I wished I'd thought of it.

Monet nodded. "She's gorgeous, too. And look at all the cleavage she's showing."

"Fake boobs," I assured her. I'd never do anything like that. Besides, Mom said not until I graduated from high school.

"I was told that the only other decent actress at this school is in Paris," the blonde said in a carrying voice. She strode onto the stage. "I'm Angie Vogel," she said. "And I'm auditioning for Katharina."

I nudged Monet. "Hey, can she do that? Just butt ahead of the rest of us like that?"

"Apparently, she can," she replied. She nodded at Mr. Fanelli, who was gushing so hard I thought his head was going to explode. "Angie, my dear, I've heard so much about you from your acting coach," he said. "We'd love to see you as Katharina."

Over my dead body.

I had to admit she did a decent reading, but there were no surprises, just a performance you could catch at any community theater in any town.

She finished her audition to a roar of applause, entirely from the guys in the audience, I noticed, and floated down off the stage.

As she walked by with her nose in the air, she said, "Try to top that." I don't know how or why, but I was sure she was talking to me. Maybe it was because she was staring straight at me.

I couldn't resist the impulse. I put out my foot and tripped her.

She went down in a heap, but about ten guys, including Mr. Fanelli, rushed over to help her back up.

"Oops," I said sweetly. "Better watch it. Where you're going, I mean."

She glared at me as she stood up and I gave her a broad smile.

Was it my fault she wasn't paying attention to where she walked?

I didn't realize until much later that Connor was one of the guys who had rushed to her aid.

I didn't consider Angie Vogel to be much of a threat, but still, it wouldn't hurt to remind everyone who ruled the junior class. I nailed my audition and then cheered loudly from the audience when Connor did a decent job with his. Honestly, I hadn't been expecting much, so I was pleasantly surprised.

Afterward, I turned to Monet.

"That went well, I think."

Monet frowned. "Not enough guys auditioned," she said. "We need a Lucentio."

"Fanelli will find someone," I said airily. "He always does."

"True," she said. "But I hope this time, he finds someone who can actually memorize his role. I'm getting tired of feeding lines to some pretty boy."

I wasn't paying attention. My mind was busy trying to figure out how to solve my own problem. I snapped my fingers.

"I'm having a party this weekend," I announced.

"What brought that on?" She raised an eyebrow.

"I think it would be nice to get everyone together. A little back-to-school festivity."

"And who do you plan to invite?" she said drily.

"Just the usual crowd," I said. "Everyone who tried out."

"*Everyone?* Even Angie Vogel?" Monet didn't even try to keep the disbelief from her voice.

"Everyone," I said firmly.

Mom never had a problem with me having my friends over, but it was a busy time at the PR firm where she worked and she'd be out of town, which was convenient. I'd have to come up with refreshments on my own, though.

Friday night arrived so quickly that I didn't have time to order from our usual hangout, Wicked Jack's.

Who knew that catered orders required a forty-eight-hour notice?

So I ordered from a new place. I didn't know much about it, but the food was within my budget and they promised to deliver on time.

It was more important, though, that I look amazing. Angie Vogel was gorgeous, but not only that, she had this way of looking at a guy, like she wanted to tear off his clothes or something. I thought it was too obvious, but they seemed to like it.

It took a trip to the salon, a new dress, and some serious heels, but I looked fabulous. The food had been delivered on schedule and Monet and I were in my living room, waiting for people to arrive.

"Don't you think we should refrigerate some of the food?" Monet asked.

"It'll be fine," I said dismissively. I didn't want to get anything on my dress.

"But the shrimp —"

The doorbell rang and I hurried to get it. There were about six drama kids standing in the door.

"C'mon in," I said. "The food is out by the pool."

People streamed in and I turned on the stereo. An hour later, we had a full-fledged party on our hands. I checked my watch.

"Where's Connor?" I asked.

"He'll be here," Monet said.

Angie Vogel walked in, and I swear the whole room went quiet. She had on well-worn jeans and an emerald-green halter top, along with impossibly tall high-heeled sandals that must have cost more than my monthly allowance. She made every girl in the room, including me, feel overdressed.

Conversation resumed as a couple of the guys in the room approached her. Some of the girls who liked girls were hanging on her every word as well.

Connor arrived a few minutes later, and I was relieved to see that he seemed to not even notice Angie as he walked straight over to me.

"It's about time you got here," I said to him. I presented my cheek for his kiss, just to let him know I was miffed.

"I had something to do," he mumbled, looking at the floor.

I decided he was sorry. "C'mon, let's dance," I said. I pulled him out into the backyard, where people were dancing near the pool.

A slow song came on, but Connor seemed distracted. He kept scanning the crowd instead of holding me close.

"What's wrong with you tonight?" I said. "You're acting weird."

"I was just — looking for Chase," he said.

"He and Vanessa have been upstairs for almost an

hour," I said drily. "Besides, since when do you need Chase with you all the time? You see him every day."

"I see you every day, too," he pointed out.

I pulled away from him to look him in the eye. "Yes, but I'm your girlfriend," I said icily.

"Sorry, babe," he said soothingly. "You're right. Let's get some food. You haven't eaten anything yet."

Angie was standing at the buffet eating the shrimp with sensual abandon when we approached. She was using so much tongue that I wondered what she would do when faced with a real live boy instead of a member of the shellfish family.

I thought it was tacky, but Connor didn't seem to mind. He couldn't keep his eyes off her.

"How's the shrimp?" I said.

"Delicious," she said. She licked her lips. "Great party."

"I'm glad you could make it," I said to her, a fake smile plastered on my face.

"I was pleasantly surprised," she said.

I wanted to say something to give her the verbal smackdown she so richly deserved, but there was the sound of shattering glass coming from the kitchen. "Excuse me a moment," I said. "It sounds as though I have some cleanup to attend to."

Someone had broken two of my mother's crystal goblets. I didn't think she'd be too upset. She'd gotten them in the divorce and had shattered a couple against the fireplace already.

I liked those goblets, though. We'd used them at every family holiday. I sighed and got out the broom.

After I'd cleaned up the mess and hidden the rest of the breakables, I went outside, but there was no sign of Connor. Or Angie.

The festivities petered out around one a.m. and I headed to bed.

I woke up the next morning to the sound of my cell ringing. Monet's number flashed on the screen. "Hello?"

"Oh, good. You're alive," she said.

"Why wouldn't I be?"

"Haven't you heard?"

I peered blearily at the clock beside the bed. It was past noon. "Heard what?"

"Half the people at your party ended up in the emergency room last night," she said.

"Hey, I didn't serve them." It was true. I knew people probably brought alcohol, but I didn't approve of drinking. Besides, I couldn't get anyone to buy it for me.

"It wasn't booze," she said impatiently. "It was the shrimp."

"The shrimp?"

"Food poisoning. I told you to put it on ice. People

have been texting all morning. Everybody thinks you did it deliberately."

"Why would they think that? I just forgot to keep it cold. That's not a crime."

"Angie Vogel is one of the people who got sick, that's why. People are saying you served tainted food to take her out of the running."

I was shocked. "I'd never do that! It was an accident. She was gobbling that shrimp like there was no tomorrow."

"Well, you'd better send out an apology, and soon."

"I will, I promise." After I hung up, I drafted a quick apologetic text and sent it to everyone who'd come to the party. I felt horrible.

I felt much better a few hours later when I found out that most people hadn't eaten the shrimp. Monet was overreacting, but to keep goodwill intact, I used the credit card my dad had given me for emergencies to send flowers to everyone who'd ended up with food poisoning. It had turned out to be a very expensive party. I probably should have listened to Monet.

Yet somehow, I blamed it all on Angie. I couldn't get over the feeling that she'd gotten sick just to spite me. Drama queen.

# Chapter 3

"What do you mean, I didn't get the lead?" I slammed my locker shut and leaned against it to glare at Monet. It was the Monday after my disastrous party, and it was shaping up to be a pretty lousy one.

"Sophie, don't be like that," she replied.

"Like what? I'd be the best damned shrew ever. Who else could play Katharina, anyway? And you know it's the only decent part in that whole misogynistic play." I blocked out the fact that Angie Vogel had Fanelli eating out of her hand during her audition.

"Who's using their SAT words?" Monet teased. She was trying to coax me out of my bad mood, but it wasn't going to happen. Not today.

"At least tell me that Connor and I are playing opposite each other," I said.

"C'mon, we're going to be late for the first rehearsal," she said, avoiding my eyes.

I stopped in my tracks. "Tell me," I commanded. I'd been certain that I was going to be Katharina. I'd been involved in drama since I was a freshman. No way would Fanelli give it to anyone else. Not after everything I'd done for the drama department.

"Sophie, keep your voice down," Monet said. "People are staring."

"Let them," I said, but I did modify my tone. I was used to the staring, but I didn't want everyone to know what I had planned. "I'll talk to Fanelli," I said. "He'll see it my way. He always does."

"I don't think so," Monet said. "Not this time. He's impressed by Angie's vulnerability. And you don't want to look desperate, begging a teacher for a role," she added.

Monet knew me too well. I loathed the stench of desperation. "What part did I get?" I said.

"Bianca," she said. She seemed to brace herself for another explosion.

"Hmm," I said. "There are possibilities there. As long as Connor is Lucentio, we'll steal the show right from under little Miss Angie's nose."

"Er, Sophie," Monet started to say, but I cut her off.

"Let's go. We're going to be late for rehearsal if we don't get moving." I linked arms with her.

Monet wasn't feeling well or something. She was having trouble keeping pace with me. If I didn't know better, I'd say she didn't want to go to rehearsals.

Kennedy High had a fabulous auditorium, and that's where we headed for the first meeting. We were a little late, but Monet was the stage manager and I was a lead. Nothing would happen without us.

I spotted Connor's blond hair. It was easy to locate him because he stood head and shoulders above the rest of the crowd. He was, as usual, surrounded by his adoring public.

"Hey, Sophie," he said. He gave my arm a friendly punch. What kind of greeting was that from my boyfriend? It was the kind of hello you'd give your soccer buddy, not your prom date. "Did you hear the good news?"

Obviously, Connor felt the same way I did, that the important thing was that we played a couple.

I snuggled into him and ignored his look of discomfort. What was with him today? "I know it's not what we planned, but I think we can make the best of it."

"Yeah," he said in a puzzled tone. "You're taking it well."

"What?" I said. "Taking what well?"

That's when I noticed that Angie was standing next to him. And the script in her hand was labeled KATHARINA.

My gaze went from her to the playbook in Connor's hand. It said PETRUCHIO.

I could feel my ears heating up. Mr. Fanelli chose that moment to walk up and hand me my playbook, marked BIANCA.

"The ingenue role?" I sneered. "I could do that with my eyes closed."

"You'll have your chance to dazzle us with your Bianca," Mr. Fanelli replied mildly.

"Who's playing Lucentio if it's not Connor?" I said, trembling with rage. I shot an accusatory look at Monet. *Why didn't you tell me?*

*I tried,* she mouthed, but my attention turned to the guy who was strolling up to our little confab.

"Sorry I'm late, Mr. F.," Dev said, smiling broadly.

I moved to Monet's side and pasted a fake smile on my face as I talked through gritted teeth. "Your brother? Your brother is playing a romantic lead opposite me and you didn't bother to tell me? You know I loathe him."

A masculine voice responded before Monet could. "Right back at ya, Sophie," Dev said. "But I'm afraid you're stuck with me."

I whirled around and glared at him. "You don't even like theater. You just tried out to annoy me."

"Don't flatter yourself," he said. "Mr. Fanelli asked me to audition. He thought he might have problems filling the role when it got out who was Bianca."

I glared at him, but he strolled over to the stage and plopped himself on the edge. He looked unbearably pleased with himself.

"Your brother is still a jerk," I said to Monet.

She shrugged. "Around you, he seems to be," she admitted.

I knew we both remembered how rotten Dev was to me in middle school, when I still had braces and baby fat. And much thinner skin.

I was a completely different person now. The braces were off, the baby fat was gone, and my skin was now as tough as a rhino's. More important, Connor and I were the most popular couple in the junior class. Everyone knew we'd be senior prom king and queen. Dev would be gone from the school by then. Just a distant memory. Oh, of course, lots of girls in the junior class thought he was the hottest senior boy, but all I saw was the guy who put a worm down my back when I was in sixth grade.

Mr. Fanelli clapped his hands. "People, let's settle down and get started."

"Monet, did you find the costumes yet?"

"Yes, Mr. Fanelli," she replied. "And they're already back from the dry cleaner."

"Kaitlin, be a dear, and try one on for us," he said. "They've been in storage and I'd like to refresh my memory."

Kaitlin got up reluctantly. The costumes must be really ugly this year.

I noticed that Connor was sitting with Angie. He said something to her in a low voice and she laughed. Her laugh matched her, sexy and confident. She had her hand on his arm and he looked like he'd just been handed a winning lottery ticket.

Kaitlin came back into the room, wearing a long, flowing gown. It was too tight in the bust and was an ugly green that made her look sickly.

Connor bent down and whispered in Angie's ear. A panicky feeling rose up inside of me.

"Those costumes are horrible," I said in a loud voice, checking to see if Connor was paying attention. He looked up. "Look at Kaitlin," I continued. "That dress makes her look pregnant."

There was a stunned silence before Kaitlin burst into tears and ran from the room. Angie got up and went after her.

"Sophie," Monet whispered, "I can't believe you just said that."

The dismay in her voice clued me in.

"You mean . . . ?"

I looked to Connor to rescue me from my own big mouth. He always saved me in situations like these. But not this time. He was looking anywhere but at me.

Fanelli was wringing his hands and looking alarmed. The cast and crew glared at me. I'd just broken the cardinal rule of high school: Never let the adults, especially teachers, know the truth.

"Could you just, for once, *think* before you open your mouth?" Dev said.

At least he only thought I was an idiot. I realized what it looked like to everyone else. That I'd deliberately tromped on the feelings of a girl everyone liked. Even worse, I'd outed her in front of a teacher.

Finally, Angie and Kaitlin came back in and rehearsals continued. I prayed Fanelli would forget about the whole thing, but I doubted I'd be that lucky.

Dev and Monet were the only people who would talk to me the rest of rehearsal. Even Connor, my own boyfriend, avoided me like I had a communicable disease.

That's when it really sank in that I would be spending a lot of time with Dev. We were playing romantic leads. I tried to remember if I had to kiss him onstage.

I was flipping through the script, looking for the dreaded love scene, when Mr. Fanelli said the words that struck fear into my heart. "Angie dear, Connor, where are you? I want my stars to spend time together and get intimately acquainted."

I swear there was a special emphasis on the way he said *intimately*. I started forward but felt Monet's hand on my arm. "He doesn't mean what you think he means, Sophie. Calm down. You know everyone is just waiting for some drama in the drama department."

I took a deep breath and looked around. It was true. All eyes were on me, waiting for a reaction. I wouldn't give them a show. At least not yet.

I watched as Mr. Fanelli led Connor and Angie offstage.

"Don't trust your boy alone with the lovely Angie?" Dev's voice said in my ear. How had he gotten so close? And how did he know what I was thinking?

I stuck an elbow in his rib and moved away from him. "Of course I do," I growled at him. But I wasn't telling the truth. I didn't trust Connor, not completely. We'd been together for two years, but I knew that he wasn't the sweet guy from the pool anymore. At least a little of his loyalty and affection was because I was considered the hottest girl in the class.

Most of the girls hated me; most of the guys wanted me. And Connor liked that. But from the looks in the eyes of the male student body, there was someone else who was piquing their interest. And she was new — as Dev would probably put it, "fresh meat," a challenge. The *x* factor, the unknown.

And me? If they bothered to burn a few brain cells or (shudder) look through our middle-school yearbook, they'd see me, complete with brace face. People had short memories, and we all had our secret middle-school shames. Unfortunate haircuts, awful orthodontia, or embarrassing bodily functions. We'd left those secrets behind, but it wouldn't take much to dredge up the memories of the old me. And then where would I be?

Not a challenge. Not a popular, gorgeous girl. Just another girl who'd managed to lose the fat and gain a good hairdresser. No mystery there. And then Connor would dump me.

Dev's pesky voice broke me out of my reverie. "Come on, Donnelly, time to get cracking."

Wimpy role or not, I did need the rehearsal time. How else was I going to steal the show?

"Coming," I said, giving him a tight smile.

We started to run our lines, reading from the playbook. I was surprised that Mr. Fanelli had chosen not to have a table read at the first rehearsal, but more time one-on-one with Dev meant that I could coach him.

Turned out that he didn't need any coaching. He was good, better than Connor. Dev had a deep, rich reading voice with actual feeling behind it. I'd always known there was more to him than a good-looking superjock, but I didn't realize he was into drama.

"Why didn't you audition for the lead?" I asked him.

"I'm *a* lead," he said mildly. "Lucentio is a plum part."

"I mean Petruchio," I said. "He's the one who gets Katharina."

"That role didn't interest me," he replied, "and besides, Mr. Fanelli asked me to audition for this part."

I was miffed that Dev hadn't been interested in the lead role. Even though I hadn't been given the female lead, everyone expected I would get it. Hadn't he wanted to work with me?

"Did you take it because you thought you wouldn't have to work with me? You could have gotten Petruchio, you know. You're good enough."

His eyebrow lifted, but he didn't comment. "Of course not," he said.

"Yeah, right," I stated.

"This isn't middle school," he said. The condescension in his voice made me want to smack him. "Some of us have grown up, if you haven't noticed."

I had noticed, to tell the absolute truth. Dev was gorgeous, dark wavy hair, tanned skin, white teeth. Connor's physical opposite, not at all my type. And now I was stuck with him and his "maturity" for six long weeks.

# Chapter 4

"But, Mr. Fanelli, you know that I should be Katharina instead of Angie Vogel." It had taken me a day to corner him, but I'd finally tracked Fanelli down in the front office.

Ms. Murphy, the principal's assistant, watched us in fascination.

"Sophie, my decision is final." His voice shook a little, but his expression remained firm. "I am the director of this production."

"Of course you are," I soothed. "But it's not fair. I've been a lead in every production since freshman year."

"And you're still a lead," he pointed out reasonably.

"Everyone knows that Katharina is the star of the show," I said scornfully.

"But don't you think it might be time for a little new blood?"

"No, I don't," I said. My voice was rising. "Mr. Fanelli, you have to give me that part," I shouted.

There was a loud snort from the front desk, but Ms. Murphy had her head buried in paperwork.

"No, I don't," he said. But he looked nervous.

"Maybe I should just quit altogether," I said loudly. Fanelli hated offstage scenes, especially ones that took place a few feet from his boss's door.

"Go ahead," he said, but I could see a little bead of sweat form on his brow. "There are plenty of girls who would love to have the Bianca role."

He was right. If I quit, he'd give my part to some other girl, probably some stagestruck freshman, just to spite me. On the other hand, the guy parts were a lot harder to fill.

"Fine, I will," I said triumphantly. "But you know, Connor, my *boyfriend,* will go with me."

"Now, let's not be hasty," he said. "We can work something out."

I moved a little closer to the principal's office and turned on the tears. "I'm just trying to do my best for Kennedy High," I wailed.

"What do you want?" he said.

I opened my mouth immediately, but he cut me short.

"I can't give you the role of Katharina," he said. "It would cause way too many problems."

I hadn't really expected that he would take the role away from Angie, but now I knew I could make a demand. "A guaranteed lead for the spring musical," I said.

We shook on it and I tried not to inhale. He overdid it on the cologne. "You're smarter than I gave you credit for," he observed.

"That's what everyone says," I replied. "See how easy that was?"

I was at my locker at lunch the next day, waiting not so patiently for Connor. We had a standing Wednesday lunch date. Juniors and seniors could leave campus for lunch, unlike the freshmen and sophomores, who were confined like prisoners to the lunchroom swill.

I was sending him a *where are you?* text message when Olivia Kaplan appeared.

"All alone?" she smirked at me. Olivia was the biggest gossip at school, and I could tell by her smile that she was dying to reveal something.

"Just waiting for Connor," I said nonchalantly.

"Oh, yes, it's Wednesday." Her eyes gleamed. "Well, I wouldn't want you to go hungry. I just saw him drive off with Angie Vogel."

Which is why she'd hurried back to rub my face in

it. I grabbed my wallet and car keys. "Oh, that's right. They're getting a jump on memorizing lines. I must have forgotten. Connor's so conscientious." I smiled at her as though I didn't have a care in the world, but inside I was seething.

"Of course that's it," Olivia said blandly, but I knew that look on her face. It was the look of a gossip hound on the trail of a juicy scent.

I was going to kill Connor when I caught up with him.

I strolled away, aware of Olivia's beady eyes watching my every move. Fortunately, Monet hadn't left for lunch yet. I caught up with her at her locker.

"Let's go to Wicked Jack's," I said.

"But it's Wednesday," she said.

I smiled at some random guy who was watching us.

"I know that," I replied through gritted teeth. "Evidently, Connor has other plans."

"Are you okay?" she said.

"Of course I am, why?"

"Because you just smiled at Jason Brady, the guy who put his hand on your butt in PE when we were freshmen. You hate that guy."

It was true. I couldn't believe I had smiled at Jason Brady. The guy was a total perv. A casual smile was like an engraved invitation to him.

"He won't bother me," I said with confidence I didn't feel. "Everyone knows I'm Connor's girlfriend."

A fact I would remind Connor of as soon as I tracked him down at Wicked Jack's and scoped out the situation.

There was no sign of him or his gorgeous costar when we walked into the restaurant. Where were they? Connor was a creature of habit and Olivia Kaplan said she had seen them leave campus. I tried not to jump to conclusions. Connor had never given me a reason not to trust him. But I wasn't stupid. Angie Vogel was beautiful, and he was spending a lot of time with her. He'd better have a good explanation.

Wicked Jack's is pirate-themed, decorated in head-to-toe pirates' booty. There are stuffed parrots, treasure chests, and even a skeleton wearing a skull-and-crossbones bandanna. Tacky, but the food is good and affordable. And it's close enough to school that we could make it back without getting a tardy slip.

Vanessa waved at us from a corner booth. "Sophie, Monet, over here," she said.

I didn't feel like talking to anyone, but I squared my shoulders and called out, "We'll be right over." Then, to Monet, I said, "Will you get me a salad? I might as well get the inquisition over."

"Sure," she said. I handed her a twenty and watched her walk off. We'd managed to stay friends even though she wasn't into the whole popularity thing and I was. I knew she thought it was silly to care so much about what other people thought, but she never made fun of me or trashed me behind my back.

The girls at the corner booth, however, were a different story. They were my couples friends, girls who dated Connor's friends. We had absolutely nothing in common, except that we were each one-half of a power couple.

I plastered on a bright smile and headed for the booth. "Hi, all," I said gaily and plopped myself down next to Vanessa.

Vanessa was still dating Connor's best friend, Chase McDermitt, who had been a total player before Vanessa organized him into submission. He still was a bit of a player, truth be told, when Vanessa wasn't around. Vanessa was also in drama, but it was only a résumé padder for her. She had her fingers in every extracurricular pie.

Everyone wrote her off as one of those bubbly blondes, but the girl was cold as ice when it came to her GPA. She was determined to get into an Ivy League school. My money was on Vanessa to make it happen.

"We were so surprised to see you here today," Haley Owens said.

Haley dated Mark Vedder, a senior. She was a junior, had a passing resemblance to Alicia Keys, and sang in every musical.

Everyone knew it would be over the minute Mark graduated from high school and left to play college basketball on the East Coast. Everybody except Haley, that is.

"No biggie," I said. "Connor wanted a little more rehearsal time, that's all. And I thought it might be fun to mix it up a little."

Connor had his faults, but a wandering eye wasn't one of them. He peppered his conversation with way too many *bro's* and *dude's*, had once eaten an entire apple pie without offering me a slice, and sophomore year, during his annual ski trip with his parents, had forgotten to call me for an entire week. That was it for Connor's faults.

Haley piped up. "I'd be careful, Sophie," she said. "Angie Vogel is serious competition. And they've been spending a lot of time together. Jason says she's all Connor talks about these days."

"He does, does he?" I said. I started to say something more, something I'd probably regret, but Monet came to the table loaded down with our lunch.

Vanessa leaned in close to me. "Sophie, I just want you to know that no matter what happens, we're still here for you."

I'd believe that when I saw it, I thought. And I ignored the rest of what she was trying to say.

"Everything is fine," I assured them. "Connor's

just excited about his role. It's a big deal for him. Who knows where it could take him? You know how important extracurricular activities are on college applications."

They all nodded in agreement, but Monet gave me an inquiring look.

As if the whole subject bored me, I speared a leaf of lettuce with my fork. "Now, what's been going on with you guys? I've been so busy with rehearsals that I need you to catch me up on the latest." But as I put the lettuce in my mouth, it tasted a little like sawdust.

Haley said, "Speaking of rehearsals, how's it going with gorgeous Dev?" She glanced at Monet and shrugged. "I know he's your brother, but he's totally hot."

Monet replied, "But Sophie and my brother have known each other forever. She's immune to his questionable charms, right, Soph?"

"Exactly," I said firmly. "Dev's like a brother to me." Monet had been burned before by so-called friends who just wanted to get closer to Dev. It was always a sore topic.

Besides, I didn't need any speculation going around about my costar and me. Not when there was evidently already enough gossip about Connor and Angie.

I'd talk to him and make it clear that his *professional* admiration for his leading lady was becoming fodder for gossip. I didn't realize that it was much too late for a heart-to-heart with my boyfriend. Matters were already well out of my hands.

# Chapter 5

That afternoon, I headed to rehearsal happily, assuming that my tiff with Connor would blow over. As I walked by the vending machines on the way to the auditorium, Alexa Campbell ran smack into me. She was eating a chocolate bar, which she managed to get all over my pristine white shirt.

"I . . . I . . . I'm so sorry," she whispered. "Don't tell my mom, please."

Alexa's mom owned a successful chain of weight-loss facilities.

"I don't need to tell your mom you're sneaking chocolate — it's obvious from looking at you." The words just popped out of my mouth.

"What a bitch," I heard someone behind me say, as (of course) Alexa burst into tears.

Belatedly, I remembered how Monet was always reminding me to think before I spoke.

"It's okay, Alexa," I said. But she just cried harder.

I ignored the mutterings behind me as I tried to console her. Geesh, some people were so sensitive.

"Here, let me wipe it off," she said.

"No!" I said. But it was too late. Now there was a huge chocolate smear across my chest.

I glared at Alexa and she started to cry again. Giving up, I went into the bathroom and dabbed at it with some wet paper towels, but the stain didn't come off. Now it was a *wet* chocolate smear.

I checked my watch. I was going to be late. There wasn't time to go back to my locker and change into a new shirt. Of course I had an extra outfit or two in there. A girl had to look her best or risk the ridicule of the world.

I squared my shoulders. Looked like it would be ridicule today, but if anyone could handle it, it was me. After all, popularity had its privileges.

Most of the cast was already onstage by the time I made it to the auditorium. There was no sign of Monet or Mr. Fanelli yet, so the volume was loud as everyone chatted or ran lines. We were supposed to be off book in a week, but some people were still having trouble.

"Hi, babe," I said to Connor. I put a hand to his blond hair and leaned in for a kiss. To my shock, he shied away.

"Uh, Sophie, we need to talk," he said.

The room went deadly silent, which should have been a clue, but I didn't catch on.

"Sure," I said. "What about?"

He glanced at Angie. She nodded encouragingly. Not one blonde hair was out of place, and suddenly I remembered my chocolate-stained, damp top.

What was going on? Since when did my boyfriend need permission from Angie to talk to me?

I looked at him inquiringly, but he was silent.

"Say what you want to say," I said, "so we can get on with rehearsal."

In hindsight, this probably wasn't the best approach, but in my defense, I had no idea what was coming next.

Angie wrapped an arm proprietarily around Connor's and whispered in his ear.

Connor cleared his throat. "True love can't be thwarted," he said dramatically.

"What are you talking about?"

"I think we should see other people," he said.

My jaw dropped. Someone in the back of the room laughed. My face grew hot and I held on to my temper with difficulty.

Angie was obviously behind Connor's sudden urge to date other people. They weren't even trying to hide it.

Rage boiled in my blood and I took a step toward her. My only desire was to hurt her as much as I'd been hurt.

I don't know what would have happened, but Dev stepped in between us. "Why don't you and Sophie take this conversation somewhere more private?" he suggested to Connor quietly. "Angie and I will wait here."

I turned and marched off into the hallway, confident that Connor would follow me. Otherwise, he would have a full-scale scene on his hands.

It was all just a big misunderstanding, I was sure of it. I was relieved to find the hallway deserted, though. I didn't think I could take another public humiliation.

That was, until Connor said flatly, "It's over, Sophie. It just happened."

"You mean with Angie," I replied. It wasn't a question.

"I'm sorry," he said, staring at his hands.

What could I say to that? I nodded, unable to speak over the lump in my throat, and gathered the shreds of my dignity. Connor didn't say anything else but rushed back to rehearsal. *To his new love, Angie,* I thought bitterly.

I waited until he was out of sight to burst into tears. I made a run for the refuge of the bathroom. It was empty, thankfully. I never thought Connor would humiliate me like this. I burst into hot tears but knew that I didn't have the luxury of a good cry. My eyes swell up something fierce and I end up with little piggy eyes. Not a very attractive image, especially if I wanted the cast and crew to think I was okay.

After a few minutes of deep breathing, I splashed cold water on my face, careful to avoid my mascara.

I was numb as I walked back to rehearsal. I hadn't seen it coming, *me*, the girl who had so carefully traversed the dangerous world of high school cliques.

Monet rushed up to me as I reentered the auditorium. "Dev told me what happened. Connor is a complete moron to break up with you in front of the entire cast like that!"

"Yes, he is," I replied, "but I'm an even bigger one for trusting him in the first place."

"Why don't you skip rehearsal tonight? Everyone would understand," she said.

I plastered a fake smile on my face. "There's no way I'm giving Angie Vogel the satisfaction."

I walked over to Dev. "Well, what are we waiting for? Let's get this over with," I snapped.

He looked at me sympathetically, which made me want to punch him.

"What's your problem?" I said. I was being a total bitch to him and it wasn't even his fault, but I couldn't seem to help myself.

Dev didn't respond to my nasty behavior. Instead,

he flipped open his playbook and gave me my prompt.

I tried to keep my mind on my role, but I couldn't help dwelling on my current situation. The breakup would be all over the school tomorrow and there would be no possibility of spinning it that it was a mutual decision. Not after the center-stage dumping I'd just received.

# Chapter 6

The next morning I woke up with a sore throat, watery eyes, and a fever.

I dragged myself to the kitchen table, where Mom had breakfast ready. I poured myself a glass of orange juice. It hurt to swallow, but I gulped it down.

"You look terrible," Mom said. "You must be coming down with something." She picked up the phone.

"What are you doing?" I said.

"Calling the absence line, of course. You can't go to school like that," she said.

"No!" I said. I would be crucified if I didn't go to school. Everyone would assume I'd slunk off to lick my wounds.

"I mean, I'm fine, Mom. And I have a test today that I don't want to miss," I lied, I hoped believably.

Mom put down the phone, but she didn't look convinced. "Sophie," she hesitated, but then continued, "is everything okay? I haven't seen Connor around here in a few days."

"Mom, everything is fine. I see him every day in school. And we have rehearsals." All of which was true. I did see Connor; I just left out the part where he was "rehearsing" with someone else now.

I would have to tell my mom that Connor and I broke up. Eventually. But I needed time this morning to get ready and if I told her the truth, I'd never make it in time.

Post-breakup wardrobe was crucial. I couldn't look like a trollop or a nun. No black, despite its slimming effects, or people would say I was in mourning.

I was kind of regretting the pint of Baskin-Robbins Monet and I had downed the night before, but it was a ritual we'd indulged in since the seventh grade when Stan Reno dumped her for a cheerleader. He'd had breath like a pit bull with indigestion, but Monet had been crushed.

"Finish your breakfast," Mom said. "And take some daytime cold medicine."

Thinking about the breakup had made me lose my appetite, but I managed to force down a few more spoonfuls of oatmeal, which seemed to satisfy her.

I went upstairs and dug out my favorite designer jeans and a turquoise top. The perfect looking-good-but-not-trying-too-hard outfit. I used about a bucket of concealer and a little bit of blush to put some color in my cheeks. Even my hair cooperated, and I went to school confident that I looked my best.

I ran into Vanessa outside before first bell. My prediction was correct. Rumors abounded.

"I just heard," she said. "I can't believe it." She dabbed at her eyes.

"Are you crying?"

"It's just so sad," she said. "You and Connor were the perfect couple. I would just *die* if Chase ever cheated on me."

I raised an eyebrow, but she looked away. I wasn't going to be the one to tell her something she probably, deep down, already knew.

"I'll be okay. Thanks for your concern."

"But who are we going to double with now? I told Chase that there was no way I would associate with that, that *home wrecker*."

The fact that Connor and I weren't married apparently escaped Vanessa's notice, but I was touched that she was on my side.

"Thanks, Vanessa," I replied. "Maybe we can do something next weekend without any guys?"

"Uh, sure," she said, but she didn't seem sure at all. There was a moment of gloomy silence and then she brightened. "Look at this," she crowed. She unzipped her hoodie and pointed to her chest. I stared at her, not getting it. Was she showing off a recent boob job? A new tattoo? No, it was her T-shirt she was proudly displaying.

"Don't you love it?" she asked.

It read TEAM DONNELLY in big, bold letters.

"All the girls are wearing them. You know, to show support after the terrible way Connor dumped you to go out with Angie Vogel."

I suppressed a groan. Vanessa meant well, but the T-shirts would just call more attention to the breakup.

"Thanks, Vanessa," I managed to reply, "but I'm fine."

She looked at me sympathetically but didn't outright call me a liar, which I supposed was something.

Still, I wasn't surprised when I saw her at lunch with her hoodie firmly zipped over her T-shirt, which made sense given that she was sitting with Chase, Connor, and Angie.

I think I would have been able to ignore it if Angie and Connor had kept their relationship low profile, but for the rest of the week they seemed to be determined to rub it in my face. They even did an interview for the school paper, for God's sake. And because Colin Jensen, the editor, was a total perv, there was a huge photo of Connor and Angie. Angie, of course, looked totally amazing.

Suddenly, Angie Vogel was Mother Teresa and a *Playboy* centerfold all rolled up in one glamorous package.

I couldn't compete. Did I even want to? I mean, I recycled regularly and there was that whole beach cleanup thing I organized last year on Earth Day, but Angie was organizing a food drive, a book drive, and a sit-in.

I admitted my feelings to Monet. "Angie makes me feel like a total dilettante. There's nothing I can do to knock her off her perch."

"She has one thing you don't," Monet admitted.

I sighed. "I know. That perfect blonde hair."

"No, silly. A boyfriend. Angie has a boyfriend and you don't. That's all."

Monet was kind enough not to add that Angie had *my* boyfriend.

"You're right," I said. "Couples rule this place. I just need a boyfriend to get back on top. Someone who makes Connor look like yesterday's news. Besides, a boyfriend would be nice. I'm getting a little sick of fending off Jason Brady."

It was true. For some reason, my stock had lowered and cretins like Jason thought they actually had a chance with me.

There had been a time when I had plenty of options, even after I had started dating Connor exclusively.

But I had never even looked at anyone else. Something I was bitterly regretting, since he hadn't granted me the same courtesy.

That was no excuse for Dev's face popping into my mind. He was the only guy whose number I had, and that was just to schedule extra rehearsals.

I was really off my game if the only guy's number programmed into my cell was my best friend's brother. How pathetic was that? Turned out it was the tip of the humiliation iceberg.

After school, Monet and I saw Hannah Johnson wearing a TEAM VOGEL T-shirt. I looked at Monet.

"She always hated you," she explained.

"What did I ever do to her?"

"Are you serious?" Monet said. "Don't you remember seventh grade? She had that mad crush on Damon and he asked you to the dance instead of her."

"That's not my fault," I said. "And it's not like I went with him."

I was happy to notice that there was only a sprinkling of TEAM VOGEL tees, compared to a solid showing of TEAM DONNELLY. Still, Angie needed to be put in her place and I had the perfect idea how.

"Monet, do me a favor," I said. It wasn't a question.

"What are you up to, Soph?"

"Never mind. Just wait and see."

# Chapter 7

Later that week, Monet and I were headed for Wicked Jack's when Dev caught up to us.

"Can I bum a ride?" he asked. "My car's still in the shop."

"Sure," she said easily.

They got along well for siblings, especially since they were only a year apart. I envied their relationship, even if I didn't understand how anyone could put up with Dev.

When we got to Monet's car, Dev sat in the back without protest. Monet pretty much just ignored him, but I was self-conscious with him in the car. I certainly didn't want to talk about my breakup in front of him.

Wicked Jack's was packed, but we managed to find a table. A couple of sophomore girls giggled and whispered when I walked by.

"Just ignore them," Monet advised.

I tried, but I felt like everyone was staring and talking about me. We'd already ordered when Connor entered the restaurant with Angie on his arm.

They took a booth opposite our table and immediately had their hands all over each other.

Now I knew I wasn't imagining the whispers and looks.

"Is he *trying* to publicly humiliate me?" I said through clenched teeth.

Dev looked up from the huge burger he'd ordered. "Doubtful," he said. "I don't think he even noticed you're here."

I glared at him.

"Not helping, Dev," Monet said.

"I can't believe him," I said. I stabbed a leaf of lettuce from my salad, imagining it was Connor's cold heart.

"Just ignore him," Monet advised.

"But he's rubbing my nose in it," I responded. My face was red, which was more fodder for the gossips.

"Do you want to leave?" Monet asked.

"Don't worry, I'm not going to make a scene."

Dev said, "I have a better idea. I'm going to get a shake."

"Hey, what about me?" Monet said.

Dev ruffled her hair as he stood up. "Already got you covered. Peanut butter–banana, right?"

Monet grinned. "You know it. Sophie?"

I tore my gaze from my ex. Wicked Jack's did have great shakes. "I'll have a strawberry cheesecake," I said. I reached for my wallet, but Dev waved me away. "I've got it."

I smiled at him. "Thanks."

Dev said brusquely, "I was just sick of hearing you cry over that loser."

I should have known better than to think that Dev was actually trying to be nice.

I noticed that several girls watched him as he made his way to the counter. He was cute, I thought. Not as cute as Connor, but cute. Too bad he was such a jerk.

Dev made his way back to us, loaded down with our shakes, but it seemed as though every girl in the place stopped him to say hi.

"At this rate, everything will be melted by the time he gets back to the table," I muttered.

"I don't get it, either," Monet said, "but for some reason, girls find him attractive."

As if Dev heard us, he broke off the conversation and came back to the table. "Here you go," he said.

I took a sip. It was delicious. I almost forgot about Connor and Angie's obvious public display of affection. At least, until he stopped by our table.

"Hi, Sophie," Connor said. "I didn't expect to see you here."

"It *is* my favorite restaurant," I said.

"Oh, yeah, I forgot."

Those few words set my temper flaring. Before I could think about it, I picked up my shake and threw it in his face.

So much for not making a scene.

Connor didn't even yell at me. He stood there and shook his head, then turned on his heels and left.

Dev muttered, "That was a waste of a good shake." But he seemed oddly pleased. Everyone else was staring daggers at me. There was an icy silence in the restaurant and I realized I'd just made a huge mistake.

On the way back to school, no one spoke.

"He deserved it," I finally said. But I wasn't sure who I was trying to convince. Nobody deserved that. My stupid temper had gotten the best of me again.

Dev snorted, but didn't say anything.

"What's your problem?" I said.

"My problem? *I* don't have any problems."

"Meaning that I do?"

"You said it, not me."

Dev didn't know how lucky he was that there wasn't another shake handy.

"Stop behaving like a spoiled brat," Dev said.

"What do you know about it?" I said scornfully. "You've never even had a serious girlfriend, and you're giving me relationship advice?"

"It doesn't take a genius to figure out what's going on, Sophie," he replied. "You don't even *like* Connor anymore. You're just pissed off that he beat you to the breakup."

I fought the tears that formed. "Yeah, that's it. I mean, just because we dated since we were freshmen? I certainly couldn't have had any feelings for Connor, right? Because according to you, I don't have any feelings. Well, guess what? I do have feelings, Dev. And they can get hurt just like anyone else's."

That was pretty much a conversation stopper. There was silence the rest of the way back to school. As soon as Monet parked the car, I jumped out and stomped away. Even class was better than spending one more minute with Dev Lucero.

The fallout hit immediately, of course. I tried to ignore the stares and whispers, which had only escalated since the scene at Wicked Jack's.

I was glad to have Monet at my side.

"So much for my theory that people would have better things to talk about," I commented while keeping a smile pasted on my face.

"You threw a shake at Connor in front of half the school. Did you really think that people wouldn't talk?"

"Admittedly, I wasn't thinking clearly," I said through gritted teeth. "Your brother has already told me what an idiot I am. But now it's time for damage control."

"Major damage control," Monet observed. She gestured toward a random freshman, who was wearing a TEAM VOGEL shirt. I glared at him, and Monet nudged me. I turned my glare into the sweetest smile I could muster.

The freshman paled and scurried down the hall. I surveyed the packed hallway. There were considerably more kids wearing TEAM VOGEL shirts today, but I tried not to make too much of it.

It was also the day that the weekly hotness poll came out. It went out as an anonymous text message. I hadn't really paid much attention to the poll in the past, but I didn't have to — I was always in the top three.

But that was when I was with Connor. I was curious to see where I stood as a single girl. And if I was completely honest with myself, I wanted to check out my competition.

Usually, it took months to get into the top ten, and some perfectly gorgeous girls at school never even broke the top twenty. But Angie was with Connor now, and I had a feeling that she'd be there, probably on the bottom rung, but she'd make a showing.

For some reason, I didn't get the text. Monet was no help. She had blocked it from her phone when we were freshmen.

Finally, I got my hands on it right before lunch on Monday. I conned a sophomore guy out of his phone by batting my eyelashes and looking woeful. He didn't look like he got many calls, anyway.

I was sitting outside with Monet at our usual lunch table when Dev came up. I quickly closed the phone.

"Can I talk to you for a minute?" Dev said.

I glanced at Monet and raised my eyebrows. She just shrugged and bit into her ham sandwich, so I got up and followed Dev a few feet away from the table, which I hoped was out of earshot. We were attracting attention, though. I saw Olivia glance our way and whisper something to Hannah. My biggest fans were keeping an eye on me.

I couldn't help but notice that Dev was looking particularly good. I wasn't the only one who had noticed. A couple of senior girls were checking him out and not even bothering to hide it.

"Sophie, I just wanted to say I was sorry. I was out of line yesterday. Your relationship with Connor isn't any of my business."

"Yes, you were out of line," I said, "but you didn't say anything that wasn't true. It was stupid of me to make a scene like that." I gave a nod toward the courtyard, where much of the school was pretending they weren't watching our every move. "You're going to ruin your reputation if you're seen with me much longer."

I was trying to pass it off as a joke, but it came off a little wobbly. Dev grabbed me and gave me a hug. "Friends, then?"

"God knows I can use all the friends I can get," I replied. "Friends it is."

He grinned. "Cool. I'll catch you at rehearsal, then." He strode off and I wasn't the only one admiring the view.

I grinned, too. Suddenly, I felt a lot better about my situation. If Dev, who was far from my biggest fan, could excuse my behavior, then I was sure that the whole thing would soon blow over and I'd be back on top.

"What was that all about?" Monet said. She sounded perturbed.

"What *what*?" I said.

"That *hug*," she said, "with my brother."

"We were just making up after our fight."

She stared at me.

"Monet, it was a brotherly hug. Like he hugs you. No biggie."

I nudged her, but she just kept staring.

"You can't possibly think that there's something

between me and Dev," I said. "I know he's cute, but he's not my type."

She gave me a weak smile. "Sorry, Sophie. I saw the two of you together and . . ."

"Jumped to conclusions," I said, with a grin.

I was relieved to have everything ironed out with Dev. He was my costar, after all, and we needed to maintain a civilized working relationship.

"Hi, Sophie, looking good." It was Tyler Berner, a senior guy who had a reputation for serial dating.

"Hi, Tyler." I smiled at him but didn't encourage him to linger.

"Are you thinking about him as a candidate for a rebound guy or something?"

I gave Monet a sharp look, then regained my equilibrium.

"He's a possibility," I said. "He has commitment issues. That's perfect for a rebound guy." I didn't want to admit it to myself, but I missed Connor. We'd spent almost every weekend together.

"According to Olivia, that's not all he has," she said wryly. "And he's been spreading it around the senior class."

"Ick," I said. I crossed Tyler off my mental list.

A tall, chubby guy from my history class approached. I searched my mind for his name.

"Hey, Sophie, can I borrow your notes from history? I missed class yesterday."

"Sure, Will. They're in my locker. I'll photocopy them and give them to you in class."

We waited until he left, then Monet said, "What about him? He's kind of cute."

I shook my head. "Total burnout. He missed class because he spends all of his time smoking weed behind the gym. Nice guy, though."

"You have options, at least," Monet said. She didn't seem to notice that none of the really gorgeous guys had approached me. But I did.

Monet and I finished our lunch without any more interruptions. My black mood lifted. There was a good chance, after all, that the scene with Connor would blow over.

Then I remembered the hotness poll and turned to the sophomore's phone. New text.

When I saw the list, my stomach took an express elevator to my feet. I stared at Monet, stricken.

"What's wrong?" she asked. "Connor post comments about your sex life?"

"No," I said. "And gross, you know Connor and I didn't... Anyway, that's not the point. The point is, I'm not in the top ten this week. Heck, I'm barely in the top twenty."

Monet was silent for a minute. "It's okay," she finally said. "Nobody pays attention to those things. You'll be back on top before you know it."

"Angie Vogel is number *three*," I said, horror-stricken. The girl who had stolen my boyfriend from under my nose was now going after something far, far more important. I squared my shoulders. She was going after my social standing. And that meant war.

Little Ms. Vogel had no idea what she was in for, because I played to win. And I didn't play fair.

# Chapter 8

The next week didn't get any better, for me at least. Kennedy was having a back-to-school dance and I was supposed to be part of the entertainment committee, along with Haley, Vanessa, and their minions. But no one ever called me about volunteering. No one called me to ask me to the dance, either.

I knew it sounded paranoid, but I felt like everyone was avoiding me. Especially Vanessa and Haley. When the signs advertising the big dance were finally hung, I knew that I'd been officially replaced. The signs were written in an unfamiliar hand — large, loopy writing that I'd bet money was Angie Vogel's.

I ran into Vanessa coming out of her fifth-period class. I gestured toward the poster hanging on a nearby wall. "Nice artwork," I said mildly.

Vanessa looked like she wanted to be anywhere

except standing next to me, but she managed to work up a feeble smile. "Hi, Sophie, how have you been?"

I raised an eyebrow. "With time on my hands, it seems."

"W-w-we wanted to call you," she stuttered, "but Haley and I thought with the breakup and all, having you work on the dance when you won't even be going to it seemed insensitive."

"Who said I'm not going?"

"I just assumed —" She faltered under my gaze.

"Well, you assumed wrong," I replied.

Vanessa smiled brightly. "Sophie, that's great news. I'm so relieved. It will make things much easier."

"Easier?"

"You know, we've been spending time with Connor and . . . and Angie." She hesitated for a moment at my expression, but then continued. "But it'll be much tidier if you have someone new, too."

"Tidier?" I sounded like a fool, repeating her every word, but my brain couldn't quite grasp what she was trying to tell me.

"Maybe we can all get together afterward. Connor is hosting the after party. It's exclusive. Just six of the top couples. And of course, you and your date."

"Date? I don't have a date." I blurted it out and knew I'd made a mistake even before I saw the pity on her face.

People didn't go solo to dances at Kennedy. Social functions were couples only, although some guys would show up without dates and try to hit on the freshman girls who didn't know any better than to show up with a group of their friends.

But top-tier girls didn't go to the dance alone. It was the rule — I didn't make it. And while I was with Connor, I hadn't even thought about it. But now I was stuck with it.

"You're going to the dance *alone*?" Olivia Kaplan's voice broke into our conversation.

I squared my chin and gave her my best icy stare. "Was I speaking to you?" Inside, I was squirming, though. It would be all over school by sixth period, with Olivia's special spin. I could hear it now. *Sophie Donnelly couldn't get a date for the dance. Poor thing. She's just so over since Connor dumped her.*

Maybe I *was* so over. Maybe whatever Connor saw in me didn't really exist. Maybe my popularity was a fluke and I belonged with the rest of the no-names who populated the campus.

I'd have to figure out something quickly. I said good-bye to Vanessa and pointedly ignored Olivia, who could barely conceal her impatience to spread the word that Sophie Donnelly was going stag to the dance.

I caught up with Monet at rehearsal. She was busy bullying Hortensio, who was played by Simon.

"For God's sake," Monet yelled at him. "Don't you know any of your lines yet?"

Simon made the mistake of muttering something under his breath. I didn't hear it, but Monet obviously did.

"No, you can't use CliffsNotes, you moron," she said. She spotted me and rolled her eyes. "Fanelli picks 'em pretty, but dumb."

She ignored Simon's "Hey, I'm standing right here."

It was the perfect time to ask her for a favor. Nothing put her in a better mood than yelling at cast members about their lines.

"I need to talk to you," I said.

"Why do those words send a shiver down my spine?" she said.

"I want you to go to the dance with me," I said. I'd never missed a school dance and I'd never *not* had a date. I was in unfamiliar territory.

"No way," she replied. "Besides, you always told me that popular girls never went alone. And also, I'd rather chew off my own arm than go to a high school dance."

"That can be arranged," I said. She looked at me.

When she showed no signs of budging, I resorted to pleading. "Please, please, please."

She sighed. "What happened now?"

"I admit it. My mouth got me into trouble."

"Again," she said. But she was smiling, which

meant there was a chance of convincing her. I could be very convincing.

Word definitely got around, though. On Wednesday, a lanky boy with stoner eyes and great hair walked up to me. "I hear you need a date for the dance," he said. His friends, who were hovering in the background, snickered.

"Aren't you a freshman?" I said.

"You've seen me around, then?"

"I think my cousin used to babysit you," I said. "Your face cleared up nicely."

He made a hasty retreat as his friends burst into gales of laughter.

"Since when do freshmen have the nerve to ask me out?" I muttered to Monet, who was barely refraining from laughing.

"Since they heard you were going with me," she replied. She was going with me with the agreement that we would put in a brief appearance and leave. She also demanded that, in exchange, I would attend no fewer than three art films and a poetry reading.

"Maybe Scott will be there," I said.

She blushed. Scott Caruso was this guy in her art class, and I could tell from the way she talked about him that she liked him.

"Cheer up. It'll be fun," I said. "I promise."

It turned out to be the farthest thing from fun imaginable.

# Chapter 9

My invitation to Connor's after party seemed to have been lost in the mail. I needed to somehow salvage my dwindling reputation, but the harder I tried to regain ground, the lower my standing sank. For the first time, I wouldn't be hanging out with Vanessa and Haley after a dance. Of course, even if I had been invited, Monet wouldn't have come with me. I think she said something like she'd rather pull out her own fingernails.

I surveyed myself in the mirror. I wore a short, attention getting red silk dress that went well with my dark hair. It had been atrociously expensive but worth every penny. I needed all the confidence I could muster for what was sure to be an hour of hell. It was too late to back down.

I grabbed my keys and yelled to Mom, who was in her home office, "working" on a Friday night. Which probably meant checking out Match.com profiles and playing solitaire.

"I'm leaving now," I hollered.

"Have fun," she said. "And be careful out there. Drive safe."

"I will. Bye, Mom."

Dev answered the door when I went by to pick up Monet.

"Sophie, come in," he said. "Where are you two headed tonight?"

Monet appeared in the doorway behind him. "None of your business."

She wore a deep purple dress and her red hair was gathered up into a cascade of curls.

Dev looked from me to his sister. "School dance?" he guessed easily. "Where are your dates?"

"No dates, just us," I said tersely.

Dev knew the rules, too, and I braced myself for a caustic retort, but he only smiled and said, "See you there."

"What do you mean by that?" Monet gave him an exasperated stare. "You never go to school dances."

"I am tonight," he replied.

I noticed then that he was dressed in khaki pants and a dark blue shirt that matched his eyes. His red hair was darker, more auburn than Monet's fire-engine red strands. All in all, Dev looked devastatingly handsome, and I wondered who his date was. I hadn't heard that he was seeing anyone seriously.

Monet pointed to her watch. "Let's get this over with. If we hurry, you can buy me a shake afterward at Jack's."

She strode out the door and I shrugged and followed her.

As we pulled into the parking lot, I spotted Connor and Angie getting out of his car. She wore a black dress, cut practically to her belly button, and had her blonde hair scraped back into a severe style. She looked like she was in mourning at a stripper's funeral, but it was a look that worked for her.

Suddenly, I felt overdressed in my red silk number. Angie had that effect on me.

"It's not too late to back out," Monet said. "You look like you're going to hurl."

"I'll be fine," I said. "I'm not going to let Angie Vogel scare me off."

I slowed down and Monet said, "Sure you don't want to change your mind?"

"No, but let's wait a few minutes before we go inside. I don't want people to think I'm stalking them."

The dance was being held in the school gym, and as we walked up, I could hear the music through the double doors.

Haley was taking tickets at the front. I handed her our stubs. "Hi, Haley."

"Sophie," she said. "How nice to see you." It didn't sound like she really thought it was nice to see me. In fact, it sounded like she wished I was anywhere but right in front of her. She peered behind me, to see who I was with, I was sure. "Oh, hi, Monet."

Monet gave her a civil reply, but I could tell it took an effort. I couldn't really blame her. She and Haley had never gotten along.

As always, there was a little cluster of freshman girls already there, hugging the wall, trying to look like they were having fun. We found a spot as far away from the air of desperation as possible.

Inside, we watched couple after couple as they streamed into the gym. Finally, a group of rowdy guys, including Jason Brady, walked in.

Half an hour later, I was standing alone. Almost as soon as we got there, Monet had been asked to dance by Scott-from-her-art-class. He was cute, despite the facial hair. And I was right — Monet definitely seemed into him.

I still hadn't seen Dev arrive, but I pretended I wasn't looking, even though the suspense of not knowing who he was dating was killing me. I could have asked Monet, but that might have sent her into a complete frenzy.

Connor and Angie weren't dancing. Instead, they

were holding court at a large table, which was surrounded by people wanting to bask in the glory of the new power couple.

I turned away. I didn't want to admit it, but it hurt to see him with someone else. I wondered if he missed me, even a little bit, or if he thought of me as this total pain in the ass he was glad to get rid of.

Jason approached me. "Sophie, would you like to dance?"

It was a fast song playing, so I didn't have to worry about unwanted groping. And it was marginally better than standing there alone.

He was an okay dancer and only tried to put his hand on my ass once. He even seemed to get the hint when I shot him a dirty look and moved away. He didn't try it again, and even muttered, "Sorry."

The song ended and Jason and I exchanged those awkward looks, the kind where you're not sure what to do next.

"Would you like something to drink?" He wasn't so bad, I thought complacently. You just needed to know how to handle him.

"Yes, thank you." I beamed at him. I was on my best behavior.

Jason was being pleasant, too, and I felt comfort knowing I had at least one admirer. I avoided glancing in Angie's direction, where several eligible guys were now buzzing around her like honeybees to a rose.

Connor looked like someone was trying to take his last cookie. Funny, it had never seemed to bother him when guys talked to *me*.

Jason was gone a long time. I waved to Monet, who was still out on the dance floor, and smiled brightly when I noticed anyone looking at me. No one approached me, though.

It had been a mistake to come. I wanted to leave, but I was Monet's ride home. I searched the crowd for Dev again. If he was there, I could ask him to give Monet a ride and leave with a clear conscience. I saw him, but he was with Beth Templeton, a senior girl, and he looked like he was having fun. I'd tough it out a little while longer.

Just as I thought for sure that he'd deserted me, Jason came back. His eyes were bright and he wore an oversize grin.

That, I thought with satisfaction, is someone who appreciates the pleasure of my company. I straightened my spine.

He handed me a cup of punch and I drank it thirstily.

"Want to dance to this one?" he said.

I nodded. It was another fast song, so what was the harm?

Back out on the dance floor, Jason grabbed my hand and twirled me. The room spun and then spun some more.

Minutes later, I was sweating profusely. We'd been dancing nonstop and more cups of punch had magically appeared in my hands.

Once, I met Connor's gaze and we both quickly looked away. I tried not to pay any attention, but I noticed that he and Angie only danced to the slow songs.

Jason handed me another cup and I drank quickly. I was having too much fun to stop and slow down.

Suddenly, I didn't feel so well. "It's hot in here. Isn't it hot in here?" I barely recognized the sound of my own voice. It was slow, slurred.

Jason wrapped his arm around my waist and held me so tight I couldn't breathe. I leaned against him, barely able to stand. He said something to his buddy that I didn't hear. The other guy laughed and they bumped fists.

He walked me toward the exit. I saw Haley give me a long stare and then scurry off. Probably to spread gossip, I thought sleepily.

"Let's go get some fresh air," Jason said and hustled me outside before the chaperones saw me.

We were out of the building when someone blocked our path.

"I don't think so." Dev's voice came from a long way off. I looked up and his face swam into view. "Sophie's not going anywhere with you." He grabbed my hand and gently pulled me free of Jason's grasp.

"I say she is." Jason yanked my arm and I stumbled.

"Look, Brady, I know what you're up to," Dev said. "Just leave Sophie alone and we won't have a problem."

"Why do you care?" His voice was pugnacious. SAT word. "What's she to you?"

I peered into Jason's face. What was I doing? I couldn't stand Jason. He was a slug. The fact that I saw two of him only underlined the fact that I'd totally blown it. Ignored all those warnings you learn in health class. You know, never set your drink down, never let a guy you don't know and/or trust get a drink for you. If you feel funny, don't ever leave with someone. That kind of stuff. The bastard.

"She's my sister's best friend," Dev replied. "And she's not leaving with you."

Jason tugged on my arm again — and that's when I threw up all over him. Pink and black vomit (I shouldn't have had two boxes of Good & Plenty for dinner) stained his shirt. I guess the throwing up grossed him out so much that he gave up. He strode off, cursing.

Dev sighed. "What are we going to do with you, Sophie?"

The fresh air revived me some, but I was still having trouble walking.

"He put something in the punch," I slurred.

"Now you figure it out," Dev replied. "What were you doing hanging out with a reptile like Jason Brady?"

"No one else would talk to me." I sniffed. Tears streamed down my face. I was still having trouble walking and now I was crying too hard to see where I was going. "What about your date?" I wailed. "Poor Beth."

"She'll understand," he said tersely. Dev threw me over his shoulder like a sack of potatoes. I was thankful that my dress wasn't any shorter, because that's all I needed, a picture of my underwear getting posted on some Web site.

Dev was strong, very strong. I clung to his back. I wasn't exactly a lightweight. Don't get me wrong, I had an okay body, but I wasn't a petite little thing like Beth, either.

He dumped me into the passenger seat of his car and took out his cell. I could tell by the grim expression on his face that he was angry. I didn't blame him. I'd managed to screw up his date with Beth, and there was a strong possibility I might barf in his car. Chalk it up to another smart move by Sophie Donnelly, the queen of popularity.

# Chapter 10

"What are you doing? Don't call my mom."

He flipped the phone open. "I'm not calling your mom. I'm calling Monet to get her butt out here and help me."

"Oh." I collapsed against the seat.

The next thing I knew, Monet tapped on the window, and then she and Scott, the art class hipster, slid into the backseat.

She took one look at me and laid into her brother. "God, Dev, what did you do to her?"

"He didn't do anything," I slurred. "Jason Brady spiked my punch. Dev saved me."

"Actually, Haley saved you," Dev said. "She saw what was happening and came and told me."

"Why you?" Monet asked what I was thinking.

"There wasn't anybody else," Dev replied. I winced at the bare truth of the statement. "I mean, she couldn't find you and she didn't want to tell Connor, so she got me."

He seemed to realize that mentioning my ex's name wasn't helping me feel any better and changed the subject. "We can't take her home like this," he said, gesturing to my mascara-stained face and my general unkempt appearance. I looked down and paled when I realized where the wet-looking blotch on my dress probably came from. Obviously, Jason wasn't the only one I'd thrown up on.

"She can spend the night at our house," Monet replied, "but I'd better call her mom as soon as we get home." She remembered her companion. "Can we give Scott a ride home first?"

I was sobering up, which was unfortunate.

"I'll talk to her," I said. "It's okay. She'll understand."

Mom didn't answer her cell, so I left a brief message telling her that I was spending the night at Monet's and not to worry. I closed my eyes and the next thing I knew, we were at Monet's.

The next morning, Monet's voice woke me up. "Sophie, it's after nine."

I was disoriented and dehydrated. I was lying in Monet's bed, wearing a pair of her pajamas. There was a bucket on the floor next to me.

The events of the previous night came rushing back to me. "Oh, no." I moaned.

"Do you feel like eating anything? Dev made breakfast."

The mention of food made my stomach churn. I felt like I'd been eating ashes or something, but I dragged myself out of bed and went to the mirror.

I looked like the main character in *The Corpse Bride,* paper-white with huge purple bags under my eyes. Somehow, this was all Angie Vogel's fault, that I'd made a fool of myself at the dance, that I had to be rescued by Dev, that I had a hangover the size of an elephant.

I stared in the mirror. I would make her pay. I just didn't know how.

I didn't even bother to fix my makeup or comb my hair. Dev had seen me at my worst already. And I wasn't trying to impress him, anyway.

Every step made my head pound, but I made it downstairs, even though I had to rest once I got to the bottom. I was never going to drink again, intentionally or otherwise.

"How are you feeling?" Monet asked when I entered the room.

"Like hell warmed over," I said.

Dev snorted. He was wearing jeans, a T-shirt, no shoes. He stood in front of the stove flipping pancakes. "You look it, too. Are you hungry?"

"God, no," I said. "Do you have any aspirin?"

After a couple of Tylenols and a bottle of water, I felt a minuscule bit better. I watched Monet and Dev eat in silence.

"Are you sure you wouldn't like some?" Dev said. "My theory is that you should eat something sugary to cure a hangover."

"You'd know," Monet said. "Remember when we were freshmen, Sophie? And Dev came home from that party completely wasted?"

"I have no room to talk," I commented.

"True," Dev said. "And at least I wasn't letting a creep like Jason Brady maul me in front of the entire school." The scorn in his voice scorched into my brain.

I glared at him, but he ignored me.

"Besides, I'm more mature now. I've learned to handle my alcohol," he added.

"Yeah, right," Monet said. "What about right before school started?"

He ignored her. "Are you sure you don't want anything to eat?"

His sister looked up curiously. "The batter will go to waste otherwise," he added brusquely.

"Maybe I could eat a little," I replied. My headache had gone away and so had the sick feeling in my stomach.

Dev made another batch of pancakes and I plowed through them.

"I was starving," I said. "Thanks."

"Do you want to hang out here today?" Monet said.

"No, thanks, I've got to get home," I said. "Mom's probably going to be worried about me."

But when I got home, the house was empty. There was a note on the fridge from Mom saying that she'd gone to the office.

I went into my room and pulled the covers over my head and slept the rest of the day.

It was dusk when I woke up, but I was completely recovered. The pancakes had done the trick.

So I thought the breakup was the worst of it. That I couldn't sink any lower. That was, until I went to school on Monday and discovered that someone *had* snapped a photo of me at the dance and sent it to every cell phone in the school — and posted it online.

I could have lived with a photo of me with my panties showing being carted off by Dev. But the photo was of a disheveled and bleary-eyed girl tossing her cookies (or candies in this case) all over Jason Brady. I don't know which was worse, the fact that the photo showed me at my worst or that I was clinging to Jason Brady.

Some smart-ass had plastered copies all over my locker. I ripped them down and was stuffing them in the trash can when Monet stopped me.

"I'd shred them," she advised. "Otherwise, they'll just hang them back up again."

She fished the photocopies out of the trash.

"How many of these are there?" I asked.

"Dev's been taking them down since he got here for swim team this morning," she said. "He called me to let me know. I tried calling you, but your cell went right to voice mail."

I grimaced. "Jason has been calling all weekend. I finally shut it off."

"He has a lot of nerve," she said, "after what he did."

"He's a cretin," I said. But my mind was on Dev. Why was he being so nice to me? The Dev I knew would have reveled in my misfortune, not tried to help me.

And who out of all the kids at the dance had taken the picture? Who disliked me so much?

As the day progressed, I realized that apparently the answer was, a lot of people. First, Hannah laughed in my face in English. Then, in PE, I was the last to be picked for softball.

"What a loser," Kent Teramoto said.

I knew he was taking about me. A week ago, he was telling everyone how hot he thought I was. Like I cared.

By the end of the day, I was steaming mad. When

I had been popular, I had never experienced so much grief from total strangers. Maybe I had ignored a few people, it was true, but I had never been mean for the sport of it.

Outspoken, yes, bitchy and temperamental, maybe, but I'd never gone out of my way to be cruel. Was that what it was like for the normal kids? If so, I was glad I'd been popular.

I didn't dare show my face in Wicked Jack's. Instead, I convinced Monet to hit Taco Bell at lunch. She didn't mind. Turned out Scott loved Taco Bell and tagged along with us.

I took a sip of my soda. "So what do you guys know about Angie?" I asked, carefully casual. "Where did she come from?"

I hadn't seen her with anyone besides Connor. And Haley and Vanessa were certainly friendly only because of their boyfriends. I needed to talk to someone who knew the entire scoop about Angie.

Monet crossed her arms. "Why do you want to know?"

"Just making conversation." I smiled at her, but she just snorted. "Scott, don't you have English with her?"

"Yeah," he said. "She and Connor sit in the back and hold hands. I think she transferred from Eisenhower."

I beamed at him. It was a start.

When Scott went to refill our sodas, Monet turned to me. "Sophie, it's a bad idea."

"What's a bad idea?" I said with studied innocence.

"Whatever it is you're planning," she replied. "Can't you just let it go for once?"

I looked at her. "You think I should let it go that she started seeing my boyfriend behind my back?"

"I heard that nothing happened before he broke up with you," Monet protested. "She wouldn't even let him kiss her until he did."

"Oh, and that makes it better? She knew he had a girlfriend. She should have walked away. Period. And then to encourage him to dump me in public — that's adding insult to injury."

"I don't think she encouraged him," she replied. "Connor used bad judgment."

Monet would never go along with what I had planned. The girl had too many moral scruples. Luckily for me, I was less fastidious.

"Maybe you're right. Perhaps I should let bygones be bygones," I said, peeping over at her to see if she was falling for it. She was. "It hurts, though."

For a second, I thought I'd oversold, but then Monet said, "You should get to know her. She's really very sweet."

I couldn't believe it. Even Monet, my best friend, obviously liked Angie. Pretty soon, Monet would be wearing a TEAM VOGEL tee, too. "I don't know. I don't think I'm ready. I'll try, though. For you."

"I could see if Angie would be open to a sit-down with you," Monet offered.

I made a face, pretending I needed convincing.

"You don't have to be friends or anything," Monet said, "but maybe a truce for the good of the play?"

I nodded. A truce was the last thing I had planned, but Monet didn't need to know that. And neither did Angie.

# Chapter 11

"Hey, Mom, do you know any of the moms from Eisenhower High?" I already knew the answer. Mom knew everybody.

She looked up from her computer. "Yes, I think Judy Blake's two girls go there. You remember Stephanie, don't you?"

"Do you think you could give me her number? I just need to talk to her about something." I didn't know what I was looking for, but I'd know it when I saw it.

"I'll get it for you," she promised. "But why do you need it?"

"Connor and I broke up," I said. "And he's dating someone who just transferred from there. His costar in the play."

She jumped up and wrapped an arm around me. "You broke up? Honey, I'm sorry."

I tried to be nonchalant but didn't move from her embrace. "It was a couple of weeks ago. I'm over it now."

She gasped. "Weeks? Why didn't you tell me?"

"You like Connor. I didn't want to tell you he dumped me."

"Yes, I like Connor," she replied, "but I love you."

It's amazing what those words can do for your self-esteem, even if they come from your mother.

"I love you, too, Mom."

"And I'm not sure I *do* like Connor anymore, if he has the bad taste to dump my daughter." She put her hands on her hips.

"It's okay if you still like him, Mom. He's a nice guy." And he was, most of the time. My public humiliation was not typical of Connor. I blamed it on a certain bad influence.

"Is there anything I can do?" Mom asked.

I smiled at her. "Just see if you can get her number. That would be great." Our moms worked together at the public relations agency, but Stephanie lived across town and went to Eisenhower.

My mom worked her magic and I had Stephanie's number within days. Unfortunately, she was out of town. Or at least I thought she was. I couldn't see why else she hadn't called me.

I spent the weekend gathering information,

looking for anything I could use against Angie, any indication that she was less than perfect.

Despite my best efforts, I couldn't find anything juicy I could use. She was gorgeous, participated in just the right amount of extracurriculars, and had hung with the popular people at Eisenhower.

I shut my laptop and leaned back against my pillows. It was going to be harder than I thought, and I like a challenge. But how was I going to find out more information about Angie? Connor clearly was in that moony delusional stage of the relationship, where the other person could do no wrong. Besides, he rarely left her side. And from the way the other guys at school looked at Angie, I couldn't really blame him. It was definitely a problem that needed some thought.

In the meantime, I needed to work on revamping my own somewhat tarnished image.

When Vanessa came up to me Monday afternoon, I was waiting for Monet outside art class — she'd convinced me to go to Dev's swim meet with her.

"Hey, Sophie," Vanessa said.

"Hey," I said. "Aren't you worried that it'll rub off?" I was still angry that I hadn't been invited to Connor's party.

She frowned. "What will rub off?"

"My complete and utter unpopularity, thanks to the dance," I replied, suddenly too tired to pretend.

"Oh, that." She shrugged. "That's nothing. It'll blow over."

"You really think so?"

"Some people at this school want to kick you when you're down. Don't you remember when that rumor floated around about me?"

I had to think about it. "You mean, back when we were freshmen?"

"Yes," she said. "You were one of the few people who didn't cough 'slut' every time I walked into the room."

"It wasn't true," I pointed out. "And besides, even if it was, you were my friend."

"Still am," she said.

There was silence as I tried to conceal my surprise. I managed to keep my normally smart-assed mouth quiet and merely smiled.

She smiled back. "Now, about the cast party," she said briskly, "do you have time to help me plan it?"

I knew an olive branch when one was waved in my face. "I'd love to."

Vanessa left just as Monet came out of the classroom. She walked out with Scott and a tall girl with multicolored hair and a Monroe piercing. She looked familiar, but I couldn't place her.

"Hi, Sophie," the girl said. "How's the play going?"

"Good, how are you?" I smiled at her, not having the faintest idea who she was.

"I went to see *Wicked* last month," she said. "I think you would have liked it. The costumes reminded me of the outfits Ms. Meeks used to wear in class."

I giggled. We had a history teacher in middle school who always wore period-appropriate clothing. On Halloween, Ms. Meeks had dressed as Anne Boleyn *after* the beheading.

"Ms. Meeks rocked," I agreed.

We chatted about the theater for several minutes and then the girl left.

"You have no idea who that was, do you?" Monet said as soon as the girl was out of earshot.

"No," I admitted, "but she does look vaguely familiar."

"Vaguely familiar? Honestly, Sophie."

"What?"

"That's Ava."

I must have still looked blank.

"Ava, you know. Ava Tate. She lives about a block away from you. Your moms used to hang out all the time when we were little."

"Oh, my gosh. That's Ava? She looks so different from middle school." The Ava I remembered was a pudgy little thing with glasses and a slight lisp.

"So do you," Monet replied.

I groaned. "Don't remind me. I was such a dweeb back then. Nobody even knew who I was."

"Ava knew who you were," she said. "And so did I."

The girl had a point.

Monet changed the subject. "C'mon, we're going to be late. Dev'll kill me if I miss his big meet. He thinks he has a chance to shave two seconds off his time."

"Is that good?"

"I have no idea."

We headed for the swim meet in Monet's car. Our school pool was being resurfaced or something, so the meet was being held a few blocks away at the city pool.

"Why are you going to your brother's meet, anyway? You hate sports," I said to Monet as we found seats on the metal bleachers.

"But I love my brother and he asked me to come," she replied. She and Dev didn't even try to hide that they got along.

"You are giving me massive sibling envy, you know. And indigestion."

I scanned the cluster of guys who were barechested in the California sun, but I didn't see Dev.

But I did see Angie Vogel, sitting in the opposite bleacher. She was with Stephanie Blake. Why hadn't Stephanie called me? I waved at her and she gave me a halfhearted salute in return.

"What's Angie doing here?" I said.

"We're playing Eisenhower, her old school," Monet said. "She probably knows someone on the team."

It seemed like she knew everyone on the team. I wondered if Connor knew where his girlfriend was. My question was answered when he showed up and took a seat next to her.

Monet nudged me. "Dev's up," she said. "And besides, you've been glaring at Angie for the past five minutes."

I don't know why, but the sight of them looking so happy made my stomach churn. I was over him, but that didn't mean I wanted my face rubbed in his obvious bliss. It was like a slap in the face every time I saw them together.

Turning my attention back to Dev, I was disappointed to note he had on a full-body-suit thing, like a wet suit.

"What is he wearing?"

"Some new swimwear," Monet replied. "Dev said it's supposed to make him faster."

"Yeah, but he might as well be wearing a muumuu for all the skin you can see. Even his chest is covered."

Monet bristled. "Why are you interested in seeing Dev's skin?"

Damn. She sounded mad. "Keep your voice down," I said, glancing over at where Dev stood with his teammates.

"You're going on about how you can't see enough of him."

"I'm not," I said, faking a shudder. "I mean in *general.*"

But it wasn't true. I wanted to see what Dev looked like in the worst way, and not in a general way but in a very specific way.

I'd never so much as looked at another guy when I had a boyfriend. Now I was practically drooling over Monet's brother, for God's sake. I seriously needed to find a date.

It was Connor's fault. Connor and Angie's. I glanced over at them and caught Angie's eye. I smiled sweetly and waved. You know the old saying, Keep your friends close and your enemies closer. It was time to get closer to Angie.

# Chapter 12

I hadn't expected it to be easy to get next to Angie, but it proved to be even more difficult than anticipated. I didn't want the whole world to know what I was doing.

I knew she ate lunch at Wicked Jack's, sometimes even without Connor, but that wasn't an option. I still couldn't bring myself to show my face there. Not after the dance humiliation, although that scandal had died down a bit, thanks to an STD. The victim was varsity cheerleader Jackie Johnson, the abstinence queen who used to hand out sexual Just Say No pamphlets at lunch.

They couldn't shut up about it in English class. We had a sub. Sometimes we got lucky and had substitute teachers who really wanted to teach, but today's candidate assigned us to read a chapter and then promptly got out his newspaper.

“Did you hear about Jackie?” Olivia whispered.

“Yes,” I said. “What’s the big deal?” Don’t get me wrong, I was delighted that the focus was off me and the debacle at the dance, but I wasn’t going to revel in someone else’s misfortune, especially not with that harbinger of doom Olivia Kaplan. I had a pretty good suspicion she was the one who had plastered posters of me all over school.

“She has crabs,” Olivia replied indignantly.

“Olivia, that could happen to anybody,” I said. “It could even happen to you.”

I didn’t think it was humanly possible, but for some reason, that shut her up.

I finished reading the assigned chapter in about ten minutes and had the rest of the period to kill. I made a list of the information I’d managed to glean about Angie.

Drama was the most important extracurricular activity she was in.

She was an only child, like me. Her parents were rich.

She’d gone to Adams Middle School.

Slim pickings as far as information went. I tapped my pencil against my teeth as I thought about my options.

Adams Middle School. That was it! I started thinking about my own hideous appearance back then. There had to be something I could use there.

During morning break, I pulled out my cell phone and dialed Stephanie's number again. I left a brief, innocuous message on her home phone. She and Angie had seemed chummy at the swim meet. Maybe she knew something I could use.

Stephanie still hadn't called by the weekend. On Saturday, Monet and I were hanging out in her room when the doorbell rang, but she didn't move to get it.

I looked at her inquiringly.

She shrugged. "It's for Dev. Beth's coming over."

"I thought they weren't serious," I said. I don't know why the thought of them alone in Dev's bedroom bothered me so much, but it did.

"They're not," she said. "I don't know what he sees in her, anyway."

"She's cute," I replied. "And athletic. So they have that in common."

"She has the personality of wet spaghetti," Monet replied. "I never thought Dev would go for the doormat type."

When we went downstairs to get snacks, Dev was sitting at the kitchen table reading a comic book.

"Where's Beth?" Monet said.

"She left," Dev said. "She just came by to get some history notes." He went back to his comic.

"Shouldn't you be studying your blocking?" I said, rejoicing in the fact that they weren't holed up in his room with the door closed.

"Got it nailed," he said. "What about you?"

"Almost," I said. In reality, I was memorizing Angie's stage moves as well as my own, which meant it was taking me a little longer.

"Give me a call if you want to study," he said. "I could always use the extra practice."

Monet grabbed a bag of Cheetos and some sodas. "Are you done monopolizing my friend?" she said.

He said, "Not quite. So, Sophie, what did you think about — ?"

He didn't finish his sentence because Monet smacked him with the Cheetos bag.

"Hey, I was going to eat those," I said.

Dev snickered. "Be my guest."

When I got home, the answering machine in the kitchen was blinking, but I ignored it. No one called me on that line.

I checked for messages on my cell, but there weren't any, yet another sign of my waning popularity. But even more vexing was Stephanie's lack of response. I mean, it wasn't like she had anything better to do than call me.

I was in my room when Mom got home from work. "Sophie, there's a message from Stephanie on the phone downstairs."

Stephanie turned out to be the information jackpot. Angie had gone to Adams with her and they had both attended Eisenhower before Angie transferred to Kennedy.

I did my nails as she talked, listening with only half an ear while she rambled on and on about how wonderful Angie was. I was trying to decide between pale pink or a bright orange when something she said caught my attention.

"And we even went to fat camp together the summer before eighth grade. I lost fifteen pounds," Stephanie bragged, "but Angie lost thirty."

*Fat camp?* I didn't have any room to talk, especially since I hadn't been exactly model thin myself in those days. Still wasn't, but I'd learned to make the most of what I had. So had Angie. But could I use it against her? I couldn't sink so low, could I?

Apparently, I could.

"Do you happen to have any pictures of you and Angie lying around?" I tried to keep the excitement from my voice.

"Forget I said anything," Stephanie said quickly. "I heard all about those photos of you that Haley Owens plastered around school. I don't want anything like that to happen to Angie."

"You heard wrong," I said sharply. "Haley is a friend of mine. She'd never do that."

"Some friend," Stephanie said. "If that's how the popular kids treat their friends, I'm glad I'm not popular."

"I'm telling you, you're mistaken. It wasn't Haley," I said, but even I could hear the lack of conviction in my voice.

"I'm sure you're right," Stephanie said soothingly.

"I am right. Now, do you have any photos, or what?"

"I wasn't supposed to tell anyone about fat camp," she fretted. "Angie asked me not to. Don't say anything, please."

I thought quickly. "I'm writing a piece about her," I lied. "It's a surprise — an inspirational piece about how she triumphed over her weight problem. It's for church."

There was silence on the other end of the phone.

We didn't even go to church, but Stephanie obviously didn't know that.

"I guess it would be all right. I'll scan them and e-mail them to you."

"Can you do it tonight?" I said eagerly.

"Sure," she said. "I'll do it right now. What's your e-mail address?"

Ten minutes later, the incriminating photos were delivered to my in-box.

I stared at the photos. One was a group shot of the entire camp. In the other one, a much larger Angie wore shorts and a T-shirt. You could clearly see the words ANDERSON HEALTH CAMP FOR GIRLS stamped across the front of her shirt.

I hesitated for about a second. Angie would know where those photos had come from and Stephanie would be in deep trouble. Angie didn't strike me as the forgive-and-forget type, but I had to do it. I told myself that Stephanie had to know that I had been lying. She was on her own.

Would trashing Angie make me feel any better? She'd been fat in middle school? So what? I had been a pudgy little dweeb. Did that mean she deserved to have her secret revealed to the entire school?

I stared at the photo. Angie's hair had been different then. Apparently, she was a bottle blonde, but it was the absolute self-loathing on her face that captured my attention. I had known that feeling well, especially in middle school.

Part of me wanted to forget about it and move on. But I couldn't. Angie Vogel was going to find out who the real queen bee was at Kennedy High. Those pictures would make sure of it.

# Chapter 13

At rehearsal, I worked the word *Anderson* into every conversation. Once I even flubbed a line and called Dev "Anderson" instead of Lucentio.

Finally, Angie pulled me aside. "Look, I know you know about fat camp."

I was stunned. I never thought she'd actually voluntarily admit it.

"I know you hate me, and maybe it was kind of crappy the way Connor and I broke the news to you."

I raised an eyebrow. "Kind of crappy?"

"Okay, it was awful," she said. "I didn't mean for him to tell you in front of everybody. I'm sorry."

"Apology accepted," I said slowly. She seemed sincere.

I was just starting to think I'd been wrong about her, but her next words changed my mind.

"Sophie, I really like him," she said. "And it's clear that you two were over before I ever entered the picture. It's just pathetic the way you're hanging on to the past."

I was fuming, but instead of reacting, I shrugged. She stared at me in exasperation before walking away. I seemed to be getting a lot of that these days.

That night, I posted the fat camp pictures all over the DramaDivas Web page. Anonymously. I made sure to post comments at every single junior and senior page I could think of. It took me half the night, but by morning, the halls at Kennedy were buzzing with news that Angie Vogel, who most everyone seemed to think was perfection personified, had been fat.

My plan was working. I was sure that the image-conscious crew known as the popular people would give her the cold shoulder. Connor might even break up with her.

I watched as she received a little taste of what I'd been experiencing the past few weeks — whispered comments, stares, and outright cold shoulders. Some people, of course, treated her just the same.

"It's working," I said gleefully to Monet.

"What is?"

I pointed to the table where Angie and Connor were having lunch alone. It was as if fat (even former fat) was contagious and they were in quarantine. To my dismay, Connor didn't even seem to notice that there was no one else around him. He was busy staring into Angie's eyes.

"Haven't you seen the fat camp photos?" I said.

Monet shrugged. "Sure, I have. What's the big deal? So she needed to lose a little weight. She lost it."

"That's not the point," I said. "The point is that when I sent those pictures —"

"Wait. *You* sent those pictures?" She slammed down her juice box. Oh, no. Monet had to be seriously angry to mistreat her juice. "Since when did popularity matter so much to you that you'd be willing to trash someone else?"

I knew she wouldn't approve, which is why I hadn't planned on telling her. She was right. I should really learn that count-to-ten-before-opening-my-mouth thing.

But Monet was too angry to listen. "I knew popularity mattered to you, but I guess I didn't realize just how much. This is pathetic."

The lunch bell rang before she could finish reading me the riot act, and I made my escape. I had a free period after lunch, so I decided to go to the library and check my DramaDivas page.

Wow, there were a lot of new comments. I scrolled down and was horrified to see how many of them were nasty. "Sophie's a bitch and we're glad Connor dumped her" seemed to be the general theme.

There was a mention of Angie's page on one of the postings, so I quickly searched for it. There were quite a few postings about her fat camp, but Alexa's was the one that caught my eye. "U R MY HERO," it read in giant purple letters.

Gag. I was tempted to post something anonymously, but I'd wait until I was home. I didn't want anyone looking over my shoulder.

"Miss Donnelly, is this the best use of your study time?" Mrs. Hubbard's voice broke into my thoughts.

"No, Mrs. Hubbard," I said obediently and signed off. I spent the remainder of my free period plotting to regain my power. With Angie out of the way, tossed firmly into the leper category, I would regain my true status.

I went through the rest of the day with a smile on my face. Even Mr. Fanelli yelling at me at rehearsal didn't faze me.

I was at the vending machine during snack when I ran into Alexa again. This time I was careful to stay well away from her grubby little hands. Still, some good PR couldn't hurt.

"Hi, Alexa," I said with forced cheerfulness.

"Sophie," she said, "have you heard the news about Angie?"

I tried to repress the glee in my voice. "I think I heard something about that. Fat camp, right? I guess she's having a hard time."

"She says that everyone finding out about fat camp is the best thing that's ever happened to her. And that she owes it all to me," she said importantly.

"What are you talking about?"

"Angie's new contract with my mother's weight-loss clinic," she replied.

"What? When did that happen?"

"When I saw those 'before' photos of her, I knew she'd be perfect for the new campaign."

"Yeah, perfect." I couldn't seem to muster a thought.

Her eyes gleamed. "It's kind of ironic, isn't it? Whoever posted all those pictures of her actually did her a favor."

"That *is* ironic." Alexa knew it was me, I was sure of it. Her next words confirmed my suspicions.

"Maybe that person will think twice before putting someone down just because she's fat — or used to be fat."

And with that, she flounced off.

# Chapter 14

Thanks to me, Angie was even more popular. She was suddenly a huge celebrity, at least at Kennedy High.

"Every time I try to regain my popularity, it goes horribly wrong," I moaned to Monet. "Why is that?"

"I don't know," Monet replied. "Karma?"

Dev showed up as we were leaving for lunch and wanted to bum a ride.

"We're hitting Taco Bell," Monet said. "So if you want Wicked Jack's, you'll have to mooch a ride from someone else."

Dev looked at me knowingly, but didn't comment. "Taco Bell's cool," he said.

Monet and Scott went to order and Dev and I grabbed a table.

"Do you want to come over on Friday night?" Dev said.

"What about Beth?" I said. Was Dev asking me out? My heart rate accelerated, then slowed. Was it a pity date?

"She has a track meet out of town," he said, sounding perplexed. "Besides, I don't think she wants to watch us prep for the play."

The play. Of course. He wasn't asking me out. I didn't examine why I didn't feel more relieved.

"I thought we could watch *10 Things I Hate About You*. It's —"

"A modernization of *The Taming of the Shrew*," I finished for him. "I'd love to."

I didn't tell him I'd seen it about ten times already.

"You'd love to what?" Monet asked. She set down her tray, which was piled high with burritos, tacos, and sodas.

I stared at the tray. "You do realize that there are only four of us eating, right?"

"Obviously, you've never seen Dev eat," she said.

Dev stretched and patted his stomach. His shirt rode up, giving me a glimpse of firm, tanned skin.

I dragged my gaze away from him, only to find that Monet was watching me. "So, you'd love to what?" she asked again.

I blushed. I didn't want my best friend to know what I had been thinking I would love to do a second ago.

"Uh, we're going to watch a movie on Friday," I said.

Monet slammed her soda down on the table.

"For the play," I added weakly.

Her face cleared and I thought I was off the hook, but a second later, she said, "Dev, I forgot the hot sauce. Could you get some?"

She watched him leave, then said to Scott, "Can you refill my soda? I'm dying of thirst."

After he left, she turned to me and said, "What are you up to, Sophie?"

I stared at her. "Nothing. It's for the play," I enunciated clearly. "Besides, it was Dev's idea, not mine. So don't think I'm trying to seduce your brother or something."

"I don't," she said, "but I don't know what's gotten into him lately. He's being suspiciously *nice* to you."

"We are in the same play together. Besides, he has a girlfriend," I stated. "And he's not my type."

She snorted. "He's only gone out on a couple of dates with Beth. That hardly classifies her as his girlfriend. And besides, I always wondered about you two."

"Wondered what?" But the guys were back, so we steered the conversation to more innocuous topics, like the upcoming test in Spanish.

The rest of the day, I thought about the conversation. What had Monet been about to say?

We didn't have play practice, so I headed for the parking lot as soon as the bell rang. I was looking forward to a night curled up with a good book. One called *An In-Depth Analysis of "The Taming of the Shrew."* Or something equally enthralling. I was looking for some help to shed light on Bianca.

I was almost to my car when I heard a honk. "Hey, sexy. What are you doing?"

I looked up and saw Pierce Hager. He was always on the prowl. I suppressed a sigh. "Hi, Pierce," I said. "Just heading home."

"Come out with me instead," he said. "We'll have a good time."

I knew what his idea of a good time was and I wasn't interested, even if he was the hottest guy in school. Which he wasn't.

"I'll pass," I said.

"You shouldn't be so picky," he said. "You're past your prime."

"I'd have to be past my expiration date to go out with a jerk like you," I said. "Now beat it."

He gave me the finger and then tore off with a squeal of tires. A minute later, I heard loud clapping. Dev was leaning against his car two rows over.

"Want to run some lines?"

When I nodded, he smiled and opened the passenger door for me.

"What was that all about?" he said as he pulled out of the parking lot.

"Pierce was just — being Pierce," I said.

"Do you get that a lot?"

"You mean guys hitting on me?"

"Dumb question," he said. "Of course you get guys hitting on you when you look like that."

"Why, Dev, I do believe you just paid me a compliment. Do you need to lie down or something?"

He chuckled, then sobered quickly. "I mean, he was kind of aggressive."

I shrugged. "Since Connor dumped me, I've been getting that a lot more than I did before."

"Let me know if someone gets out of line," he said. "I'll take care of it."

"I can take care of myself," I said sharply, then added, "thanks, though."

"Should we go to my house?" he said. "Monet's at Scott's."

"Why don't we go get a coffee somewhere?" I suggested. I could imagine Monet's reaction if she came home and found me at her house alone with her brother.

"Coffee it is," he said. A few minutes later, he pulled into a Starbucks parking lot.

The place was deserted, so I grabbed a table while Dev ordered the coffee. When he came back, we opened our scripts and got to work.

Two hours later, I noticed the time. "I've got to get home," I said. "Mom will kill me if I miss dinner."

He drove me back to the school parking lot and waited for my car to start. I gave him a wave to signify I was okay, but he stayed put.

"I'll follow you home," he said.

We lived in a safe neighborhood, but it didn't hurt to be careful. I nodded.

As we pulled out of the parking lot, I noticed Olivia Kaplan's car was still there and wondered what she was doing at the school at this time of the night.

I pulled into my driveway and gave Dev another wave.

"Don't forget about tomorrow night," he said before driving off.

Forget about it? I couldn't wait.

# Chapter 15

As I got ready on Friday night, I told myself it was just Dev and it wasn't a date, it was research, but there were still butterflies floating around in my stomach.

"Mom, I'm going over to Monet's," I said. Except, of course, Monet wouldn't be there.

"Oh, that's nice. I'm going out myself. I'm meeting a friend for drinks. Tell Monet I said hi."

A friend, huh? She sounded distracted. Was it possible that my mom had a date? She hadn't dated much since the divorce.

When Dev answered the door, I realized that a date with me really was the farthest thing from his mind. He was wearing holey jeans and a ratty old T-shirt, and was barefoot. He still looked devastatingly attractive and I had to remind myself that I was there to study my craft, nothing more. Still, I was glad that I had dressed down in a *Wicked* T-shirt and faded (but still flattering) jeans.

"I'm glad you're on time," he said. "I already went to the video store. I rented *10 Things I Hate About You,* but the guy at the counter recommended this old movie called *Kiss Me, Kate,* so I got that, too. He said it's another retelling."

Dev actually wanted to spend four hours with me?

"I'll make some popcorn," he said. "Meet you in the family room."

I knew Dev had a television and DVD player in his room. It wasn't that I wanted to be alone in his bedroom, but I was a little miffed that, apparently, neither did he. I reminded myself that I was no longer the hottest girl in school. Or, if the newest poll was true, even in the top twenty.

There was no sign of Mr. and Mrs. Lucero. Monet and Dev's parents traveled a lot, so it was possible they were gone for the weekend.

Monet and Dev never had any parties, though. They said they'd get killed, but I think the truth was that they plain old didn't want to disappoint their parents.

I debated about where to sit, but Dev had already placed a couple of sodas on the coffee table in front of the soft, squishy couch.

"Do you like butter on your popcorn?" Dev shouted from the kitchen.

"The more the better," I replied. After all, I wasn't trying to impress him.

Dev came back with a big bowl of popcorn and a bag of mini Hershey's. He sat next to me. I jumped a little when he reached behind me, but he was only shutting off the lamp on the table behind the sofa.

If he noticed my skittishness, he didn't comment. "Which movie do you want to watch first?"

"*Kiss Me, Kate,*" I decided. Funny, Connor had never asked my opinion. He didn't mean anything by it, but I was realizing it was nice to be consulted.

At first, I couldn't relax. I was hyperaware of Dev's body so close to mine, but as the movie progressed I relaxed.

I suppressed a yawn.

Dev handed me a soda. "Too many late nights?"

"Of course not," I said. "Haven't you heard? I have no social life."

"This is social," he said. He pointed to the junk food spread out on the coffee table. "Dinner and a movie."

"You're a cheap date," I observed. "I mean—" I clapped my hands over my mouth. "I don't m-mean . . ." I stuttered.

"Relax, Donnelly," he said. "I know what you meant." He leaned back and draped his arm over the back of the couch.

I finally did relax. I'd known Dev forever, and his

days of putting worms down my back were over. Popcorn, however, was another matter.

A kernel of popcorn somehow made its way down my back. His fingertips brushed against my bare skin and I shivered.

"Hey," I said. "I thought your bratty days were behind you."

He grinned. "Evidently not." He threw another kernel down the back of my neck.

I scooped up a handful of popcorn. "You're in for it now, Lucero." I reached over and dumped it in the front opening of his shirt.

"Watch the threads," he teased.

"Because that's your good shirt?" I mocked him.

"Because it's my favorite shirt," he said.

"Too bad," I said. "You started it."

Suddenly, it was an all-out popcorn fight. I laughed hysterically as I volleyed popcorn at his head.

He retaliated by running to the kitchen. He returned with a cupful of ice.

"Not fair," I said as he advanced.

He moved in as close as a kiss, and suddenly, my breathing slowed. His eyes warmed. Neither of us looked away.

"Sophie," he said. He leaned in closer.

"What's going on here?" Monet's voice interrupted.

I inhaled, still caught in Dev's gaze.

He put the cup down and reached for the remote. "We were taking a break. Want some popcorn?"

I couldn't meet Monet's eyes. I was almost sure Dev had been about to kiss me. And I was completely certain I would have kissed him back.

Dev started *10 Things I Hate About You* and Monet plunked herself between us on the couch. She didn't say a word, but I could tell she was mad at me.

It was almost midnight when the movie ended. I yawned again.

"I didn't see your car outside," Monet said. It was the first thing she'd said to me in an hour. Halfway through the movie, she'd asked me to pass her the candy, but that was it.

"I walked," I explained.

I expected Monet to ask me about that, but instead she gave me a level stare.

"I should be getting home," I said.

"I'll give you a ride," Dev said.

Monet made a furious little noise.

"No, that's okay," I said. "I can walk back. It's only a couple of blocks."

"I'll drive you," Monet said. "I want to talk to you, anyway."

I met Dev's eyes. We both knew we were in trouble.

# Chapter 16

She pulled into my driveway and cut the engine. "Please tell me you are not interested in my brother," she said.

"We're just friends," I said. "I thought you'd be happy we're getting along."

"It looked like you were getting along all right," she said. "And he was wearing his lucky jeans."

His lucky jeans? What did that mean? They certainly fit him well. I fanned myself with my hand. "Is it hot in here?"

"No, it's not," she said. "And quit changing the subject."

"We were just improvising," I said. I met her eyes, but it took an effort. I didn't like lying to my best friend, but what choice did I have?

"Good," she said, "because Scott has this friend —"

I groaned. "Now I'm so pathetic that my best friend has to set me up on a blind date? No way."

"He's really nice," she said. "He has a great—"

"Don't you dare say personality," I warned.

"Smile," she finished. "And he's blond and athletic. Totally your type."

"What's the catch?" I wasn't sure a Connor clone *was* my type any longer.

"What do you mean?"

"I mean, what's wrong with him? Why is he on the market?"

"He's a freshman in college. His name is Tanner. He broke up with his girlfriend a couple of months ago. They tried the long-distance thing, but it didn't work. He works with Scott at the art supply store."

"Can I think about it?"

"Of course," she said. "But, Sophie, don't wait too long. You've got to get over Connor sometime and get back into dating."

"Is that what everyone thinks? That I'm pining over Connor?" The thought horrified me.

"Maybe," Monet said. "You know how people are."

"Hmm. Maybe a college boy *is* just what I need." I felt a thrill of satisfaction at the thought. I'd been momentarily distracted from my goal. A college boyfriend could do a lot to prop up my fading status.

"Scott and I are going out tomorrow night," Monet said. "We'll probably catch a movie. You and Tanner could go with us."

I nodded. "Can we have dinner at Wicked Jack's first?" We were bound to see some of the kids from school there, which would get the rumor mill going and, hopefully, start mending my broken reputation.

It had been a long time since I'd been on a first date, so it was natural that I was nervous. Tanner and Scott were meeting us at my house. Nice guy or not, I needed to meet him on my own turf. I was still skeptical that Tanner was a great catch. Why was he willing to date a high school girl? And why would he need a setup? Then again, why did I?

I bounced on my bed and checked my watch.

"Will you relax, already?" Monet said.

"What if he doesn't like me?" I said. "Or worse, what if he's a troll?"

"He's not a troll."

I ignored her comment. "If he's a troll, we're not going to Wicked Jack's," I warned.

"He's not a troll, I promise."

She was right. He was definitely not a troll, at least not on the outside.

I gave him the once-over as Monet introduced us. He was taller than Connor, I noticed with satisfaction. Blond hair, blue eyes, broad shoulders. Pretty much the epitome of my type, so why did I feel like something was missing?

"Where would you like to go for dinner?" Tanner said politely, after we'd exchanged a few pleasantries.

I met Monet's eye and winked. "Monet and I thought we could go to Wicked Jack's."

Scott groaned, but he didn't complain.

On the ride over, I asked Tanner a few questions: major (undeclared), sport (baseball, like Connor).

Finally, I decided to ask straight out what I really wanted to know. "What made you agree to go out with me? I mean, you're in college. I'm sure you could have your pick of girls."

He blushed. "Uh, I saw a picture of you. Scott mentioned that you'd recently broken up with your boyfriend. So we have that in common."

"You recently broke up with your boyfriend?" The words came out before I could restrain myself. As usual.

"Huh?" he said. His face clouded over.

Poor Tanner was dumb as a stump. It was becoming clear to me now.

"Never mind," I muttered. "Do you still talk to your ex much?"

"Every day," he said.

I lifted an eyebrow.

"We're still good friends," he said. "And I miss her. You look a lot like her. Annabel has the sweetest disposition."

I hoped Monet could hear this in the front seat. She'd set me up with a lovelorn fool who thought I looked like his ex. And I thought he looked like *my* ex.

I suppressed a caustic comment with difficulty. We were almost at Wicked Jack's. No time for the reply dancing on my tongue. I needed to give the impression that everything was peachy.

The restaurant was packed. I smiled at Tanner sweetly and wrapped my arm around his bicep. I gave the impression that I was absorbed in his every word, but my eyes scanned the room. Who was there?

Olivia Kaplan, sitting at a booth with Hannah and a bunch of their friends. Good.

Connor and Angie, sitting in a dark corner. Angie looked amazing in a simple green dress. A little much for the restaurant, but judging by the way Connor had his tongue down her throat, he didn't seem to mind.

I waved to Ava, who was sitting with a bunch of kids from Monet's art class.

My stomach lurched when I met Dev's eyes. What was he doing at Wicked Jack's on a Saturday night? He was with the guys from the swim team and didn't see the little wave I gave him. Beth was giving him the eye from a table a few feet away. Stalker, much?

I was one to talk, I know. Of course, I picked Wicked Jack's because I knew Connor would probably be there. He was a creature of habit, utterly lacking in originality. It had never bothered me before, but now Connor's little flaws were getting on my nerves.

All the tables were full, so we had to wait for an opening.

"I'm starving," I said. "Let's wait over here." I headed for a table of freshman girls. It was clear from the pile of empty dishes that they'd been there for a while. I gave a little blonde an icy stare and she practically leaped to her feet.

"Behave yourself," Monet hissed, "and quit terrorizing the freshmen."

"I didn't do anything," I protested. "Besides, they were finished, anyway."

Five minutes later, the table had been bused and we were seated.

I craned my head, pretending to look for our server, but I was really checking out the reaction of the room. Olivia and Hannah were practically doing a Linda Blair to see who I was with.

Dev was glaring at me. I gave him another wave. "Your brother's here," I said to Monet. "Let's go say hi to him."

She stared at me. "Why would I want to do that? I see him all the time." She gave me a suspicious look. "What's up with you?"

I leaned in. "He's sitting a few tables away from Connor."

"So?"

"So I want Connor to see me here with Tanner," I explained.

"Hi, Sophie." I jumped. Connor was standing at our table. There was no sign of Angie.

"Why, hello, Connor," I said.

Connor stuck out his hand to Tanner. "Connor Davis," he said. "I'm Sophie's —"

"Connor and I are in a play together," I interrupted. "With his girlfriend, Angie."

Who, I saw from the corner of my eye, was looking decidedly grouchy, sitting alone at their table.

"This is my friend Tanner," I said to him. Connor's eyes focused on Tanner's arm, which was casually draped over the back of my chair.

"You look familiar," Connor said. "Do you go to Eisenhower?"

Tanner smiled. "No, man. The university."

Connor cleared his throat. "Oh. How did you and Sophie meet?"

Tanner started to answer, but I cut him off before the words *blind date* could cross his lips.

"Monet and Scott introduced us," I said. "It appears Angie is trying to get your attention," I added.

Connor didn't budge from our table. "How long have you two been going out?" he persisted.

A soft voice broke into our conversation. "Connor, our food is here." Angie stood at our table in all her glory. I gauged Tanner's reaction. He wasn't staring or drooling or anything else the boys at my high school did at the sight of Angie.

"Hi, Angie," I said politely. "Would you like to join us?"

Connor looked alarmed at the suggestion. "Go on back to the table. I'll be there in a minute, babe."

She didn't budge.

"Connor, I wanted to get to know your new girlfriend a little better," I said.

Angie flinched.

Unfortunately, our food arrived then and Connor finally retreated to his own table, with Angie trailing in his wake.

"That wasn't awkward at all," Monet commented wryly. "And what was that all about? You can't stand Angie."

"Just trying to be friendly," I said. I fiddled with my napkin to hide my expression.

"That was your ex, huh?" Tanner said. Maybe he wasn't so dumb after all.

I nodded.

"Seems like a nice guy," he continued.

I took a bite of my pasta and smiled at him. It had been a very successful first date. I could see it in the faces of my classmates. I was on my way back to the top.

# Chapter 17

I walked into rehearsal on Monday with a renewed sense of confidence. I could face Angie and Connor again with my head held high.

The date with Tanner had gone well, the biggest mouth in school had seen us together, and I detected a thaw in the air. Hannah actually said hi to me in English class, and there was no sign of her TEAM VOGEL T-shirt.

Monet was already there and she'd wrangled Ava and Scott into helping with the sets.

Connor and Angie were there, too, but I didn't let their lack of discretion bother me. They could cuddle and kiss all they wanted. Sophie Donnelly was making a comeback.

"Hi, are you ready to work?" I said to Dev, who was helping carry scenery.

He grunted in response and stalked off.

"What's wrong with him?" I asked Monet.

"No idea," she said.

I shrugged. "Nothing can get to me today. You were right. Going out with Tanner was smart."

"He's a nice guy."

I shrugged. "He's certainly good-looking, and that is definitely helping me get back on top."

"I didn't set the two of you up so that you could use him to become popular again."

"So why did you?" I was annoyed. Monet was acting as though I was committing a crime or something. "I've never made a secret of the fact that I like being liked."

"Being popular doesn't necessarily mean you're liked," Monet snapped.

"What are you talking about?" The idea stopped me in my tracks.

"Ask yourself why being popular is so important to you."

Ava came over. "Monet, where should I put this?" She had a painting of a Tuscan villa in her hands.

"Ava, that's gorgeous," I said.

"Thanks," she said. "I painted it from a photo I took when we went on vacation there last summer."

Mr. Fanelli clapped his hands. "All right, places, everyone. And remember, people, you need to be off book. You've had four weeks to memorize your lines. I'm going to start imposing fines on Monday."

Most of the cast groaned, but I smiled smugly. I had a gift for memorization and had both Bianca and Katharina down cold.

"Sophie, Dev, where are you? I'd like to work with the two of you."

"I'll get him." I finally found Dev in the closet where the crew kept the supplies they needed to design the sets. I observed him for a minute as he hoisted cans of paint onto the shelf. The muscles in his arms rippled. Just then, he turned around and caught me staring.

"Fanelli wants us," I said.

"I'll be right there," he said.

I hesitated. "Did I do something wrong?"

"No."

"Because you're acting like you're mad at me about something."

Dev ignored the question. "C'mon, Fanelli is waiting."

"Let him wait. You didn't answer my question."

"Sophie, why do you have to be like this? Just when I think I . . ." His voice trailed off.

"You what?" I said. Butterflies were building in my stomach. "What, Dev?"

"Never mind," he said. "I'm not in the mood to stand in line to worship the great Sophie Donnelly."

"Nobody asked you to," I snapped.

Monet poked her head into the room. "Mr. Fanelli

is asking where you two are," she said. "He's almost at the hissy-fit stage. He's muttering something about spoiled little prima donnas."

"We all know who he's talking about," Dev said, shooting me a glare. He strode off.

"Your brother has a serious case of PMS," I said.

Monet was smiling. "It's good to see that nothing's changed with you two."

As we walked back to rehearsal, I wondered. Something had definitely changed between Dev and me, but what?

Monet caught up with me the next day before class. "Hey, you had fun the other night, right?"

"You mean with Tanner? Yes. In fact, I was hoping he'd ask me out again."

"That's great," she replied. "Because both he and Scott have to work on Friday night until closing and they wanted to know if we wanted to do something afterward."

"Why didn't he ask me himself?" I said.

"He's shy," she said.

"Sounds good," I said. And it wasn't like anyone else was beating down my door. I had to have some kind of social life or people would think I had turned into a recluse or something.

But on Friday, I was in the library during free

period when Eli Hudson, a big-man-on-campus senior, leaned over to me from the next table. "Hey, Sophie," he said. "My parents are out of town for the weekend. I'm having a party tonight."

It was the break I'd been looking for. I hadn't been invited to an A-list party in weeks and Eli was a genuinely nice guy. Tanner was a dead end. Pretty, but not the sharpest crayon in the box.

But with Eli, there were definite possibilities. Going out with him would be a coup. I was pretty sure he wasn't seeing anyone.

I glanced over at the librarian but she was busy updating her blog or something. I gave him a flirtatious smile. "I'll be there," I said.

His smile was sincere. "Looking forward to it."

I didn't care that our imaginary romance was bound to be short-lived, since he was a senior. In my mind, we were already an item. We'd meet at the party, connect, he'd ask me to Homecoming, we'd date his senior year, and then understandably, he'd break up with me right before he left for college.

I was so busy daydreaming about my future with a guy I barely knew, it completely slipped my mind to tell Monet that my plans had changed.

I spent hours on my hair and the perfect outfit. Eli and Connor didn't exactly run in the same crowd, but they did have mutual friends, so it was possible that he and Angie would show up at the party.

I drove to Eli's house and had to park three blocks away. There were cars everywhere, but I didn't see Connor's.

I took a deep breath and walked up the front steps.

A couple of kids from my history class waved to me, and someone handed me a red plastic cup full of some unidentifiable liquid. I discreetly dumped it in a potted plant when no one was looking. Too late, I realized it was a silk plant.

As soon as I entered the living room, my dreams of a romance ended with a sickening crash. Eli was already horizontal on the couch with Madison Elliot. How could I have ever been interested in him? Madison was a freshman, for God's sake.

I wandered around the house. There were plenty of people I knew, but nobody I really wanted to talk to.

"What are you doing here?" Dev's voice said in my ear. "I thought you had a hot date tonight?"

"What?" I said. "Oh, no! Please don't tell Monet. I *completely forgot*."

"You're asking me to lie to my own sister?"

I looked meaningfully at the beer in his hand. "Tsk-tsk. What would Barbara and Herb think of their eldest son drinking?"

"Now you're going to blackmail me," he said. But he didn't sound that upset. In fact, he made it sound like something deliciously depraved.

Before I could answer, my cell rang and I picked it up without checking the number. I could barely hear over the noise of the party.

"Where are you?" Monet's voice crackled through the line.

"What? I can barely hear you."

"You were supposed to meet us at the art supply store, remember? Tanner's been waiting for you for over an hour."

She'd kill me if she knew where I really was. I pushed the mute button and headed for the door.

Once I was safely outside, where the noise level was considerably lower, I clicked the button again. "Monet, I'm so sorry. Please tell him I don't feel well."

"You're never sick," she said suspiciously. "And what's all the noise in the background?"

"The neighbors are having a loud party," I lied. "It's keeping me up and I have a terrible headache." And suddenly, my temples *were* throbbing. It was stressful to lie to my best friend.

I don't know what came over me to lie. Dev had already seen me. There was no way he wouldn't rat me out to his sister.

But when I went back into the house, he had disappeared. I wondered if he was there with Beth, but I didn't catch sight of them.

I squared my shoulders. I had come to the party in order to find an eligible guy. It obviously wasn't going to be Eli, but there were plenty of other eligible guys, most of them seniors.

In fact, I spotted Chad Laughlin sitting near the keg. He was good-looking and charming, and we'd been in several drama productions together. Unfortunately for him, he had broken his leg skateboarding right before tryouts. He'd do nicely.

"How's the leg?" I sat next to him on a folding chair. I put my hand on his arm, but he moved away to fill a red plastic cup with beer and handed it to me. I hated the taste, but sipped it for courage.

He handed me a Sharpie. "Wanna sign my cast?" he asked.

"I'd love to," I trilled. I was so out of practice with flirting. My mind raced, trying to think of something witty to write. Finally, I decided that blatant was the way to go, so I just signed my name and scribbled "call me" and my phone number.

He peered at the words blearily and then began to chuckle.

"Oh, I'm a joke now? Thanks a lot, Chad. I thought you were a nice guy." I got up, but he caught me by the arm.

"Sophie, I'm sorry," he said. "I wasn't laughing at you. I'm laughing because — well, your timing couldn't be worse."

Mollified, I sat back down. "And why is that?"

"I would have loved to go out with you. My dad would have loved you."

I gave him a puzzled look.

"Where were you when I was still in the closet?" he said.

"Closet?"

"I'm gay," he said. "And I just told my parents last week. They didn't take it very well."

"I'm sorry to hear that," I said.

He drained his glass. "Yeah, me, too."

I couldn't bring myself to work up the courage to try again and we spent the next half hour hanging out while I caught him up with what was going on with *The Taming of the Shrew.*

"So you and Connor broke up, huh?"

I nodded. "Being single sucks," I said.

"You said it, sister," Chad replied. He tapped his glass against mine.

For some reason, maybe because of my lack of success with Chad or because Eli and Madison seemed to be trying to make out on every available flat (and not so flat) surface in his house, the party had lost its sparkle. Besides, it was always best to leave 'em wanting more, so I took off.

Monday at school, I was riding high until I saw Monet walking toward me in the hallway. One look at her face and I knew I was in trouble. She was seriously pissed off.

Still, I was shocked when she said, in a low voice, "You and I are no longer friends."

"Why?"

She looked at me levelly. "You know why."

"I can't believe Dev told you."

"Dev? What does Dev have to do with this?"

"N-nothing." For a minute, I thought that it wasn't about the party, but her next words robbed me of that notion.

"Eli's party," she said. "You stood Tanner up so that you could go to Eli's party. And I worked so hard to convince him —"

"I'm sorry. Let me explain — hey, wait a minute. Convince him of what?"

She had been about to say "convince him to go out with you," I was sure of it.

"Convince him that you were a nice girl," she replied. "And then you do this. We're done." She started to walk away.

I caught her arm. "You have to give me another chance. You're my best friend."

"We're only friends when it's convenient for you," she said. "You're not ever really there for me. You're always so busy trying to become some sort of It girl that you barely even listen to me anymore."

"You're just mad about the Eli thing," I replied. "I told you I was sorry."

"It's not just about that," she said. "You've always liked being popular, dragging me along to hang out with those phonies."

"You never said anything," I replied.

"Oh, I said things," she said. "You just never listened."

"We can do whatever you want," I said. "I promise you I'm trying."

She softened a smidge. "Art museum on Sunday, and you have to call Tanner and apologize."

I had called Tanner to apologize, but we both knew that there wasn't anything between us. Even simple, sweet Tanner had figured that out.

# Chapter 18

I went to rehearsal feeling pretty good, until I saw Connor and Angie onstage. Then it hit me. She had everything that should have been mine. My boyfriend, my popularity, and, most important, my role.

Just then, Connor swept her into a passionate kiss.

"That definitely isn't in the script," Monet muttered.

"It's hot, though," Olivia said. Her eyes gleamed. I could tell she was bursting to spread the word about Connor and Angie's hot lip-lock as soon as rehearsal ended.

The whole cast was watching, enthralled, as they continued to make out.

"Where's Mr. Fanelli?" I said. "He can't seriously be allowing this. It's practically porn."

But no one was listening. The entire cast ignored me. It was as though I wasn't even there, and I realized that this was what most kids went through every day, being invisible. I didn't like it.

Tears were forming, but I blinked them away. I thought I was over Connor, that it was just about the popularity, but it hurt to see him so into Angie that he didn't even notice anyone else. He'd never felt like that about me.

It was too much to bear. I ran from the auditorium and headed for the costume room to mope in peace. I was sure that someone would notice I was gone, but I was wrong.

I cried until my eyes were swollen and my nose was running. Which was horrifying when I realized that someone had followed me. Dev.

"Sophie, are you all right?" I heard his voice from the hallway and ducked behind a rack of costumes.

"Sophie, I know you're in there," he said in a gentle voice. His footsteps grew close.

"Go away, Dev."

"Come on out of there," he said. "I'm not leaving until you do."

I frantically tried to erase the signs of my weeping. A second later, the costume I was hiding behind was pushed aside and Dev appeared.

The expression on his face caused me to promptly burst into tears again. He took me into his arms. My face was pressed against his shoulder and I prayed that my nose wouldn't run on his shirt.

At first he held me for comfort, but then he put a finger to my chin, lifting it and forcing me to look directly into his eyes. He kissed away a tear trailing down my cheek. His lips moved to the corner of my mouth. The kiss deepened.

We kissed passionately. Part of my brain was processing the fact that I was kissing my best friend's brother and screaming *bad idea*, but the other part of my brain, the part in control, was marveling at the splendid way Dev kissed.

Somehow we tumbled to the floor, landing on a pile of discarded clothing. A foggy part of my brain knew we should stop, but somehow, instead, my hands were caressing his back when the door opened.

My eyes snapped open, dreading that I would see Monet. Instead, Olivia Kaplan stood in the doorway. She met my eyes and then, with a smirk, slowly backed out of the room.

Dev didn't notice. I stiffened, suddenly realizing the enormity of what we were doing.

I put a hand to Dev's chest and pushed him away.

"We should get back," I said, "before someone misses us."

Besides, I needed some time to figure out what was going on.

He reluctantly agreed. He gave me one last kiss and helped me to my feet. "I'll see you later."

I watched him leave. What did that mean? "I'll see

you later?" "I'll *call* you later?" Or "Thanks for the seven minutes of heaven but I don't want to be seen in public with you"? Either was a possibility.

I sat back down and contemplated the sad state of my love life when I worried if a guy was blowing me off or not. The old Sophie would have been completely sure of herself, certain that the lucky guy would be on the phone before the sun set.

I realized I was sitting on one of the costumes for the current production. It must have fallen off the metal rack they used to take the costumes back and forth to the dressing rooms.

When I looked at the rich red silk costume, I wanted to throw something.

On impulse, I grabbed it off the hanger and tried it on. It looked fabulous on me. And who knew? If something happened to Angie and she was unable to perform, I could step in. We weren't exactly the same size, but it fit. It was a little tight in the bust, but not enough to be a problem. And I'd been secretly memorizing Katharina's part along with Bianca's for a reason, after all.

Way in the back, I found a section of clothes from when the school did *Oklahoma!* a few years ago.

Next, I tried on the costume Haley had worn when she'd screeched out "I Cain't Say No." Despite her resemblance to Alicia Keys, Haley didn't have Alicia's pipes. I took it off and then hung it back up carefully.

I don't think *anyone* in the drama department wanted to revisit *Oklahoma!* after Haley's performance.

Next, I found a gorgeous blue flapper costume. I didn't know what production that was from, but trying everything on made me remember how much I loved acting, being able to slip into someone else's skin for a few hours and make an audience believe I was somebody else.

I exited the costume closet feeling pretty satisfied with myself. I looked both ways, but the hallway was empty.

The auditorium was empty, too. Rehearsal had ended, but it looked like no one missed me. I breathed a sigh of relief. Maybe I could alibi my way out of what was sure to be gossip tomorrow. I was in rehearsal the whole time.

But unfortunately, Monet had noticed my absence. My phone rang as soon as I made it home.

"Hey, I'm sorry about today," she said. "I started to go after you, but then Fanelli had a crisis and I had to take care of it."

"No big deal," I said.

"Are you sure you're okay? You sound funny."

"Just a long day."

"Where did you disappear to?"

"I holed up in the costume closet and tried on some costumes. Alone," I added quickly.

"Don't let them bother you," she said. "Have you heard from Tanner lately? Scott and I thought we could all hang out at the gallery this weekend."

It was on the tip of my tongue to confess, honestly. She was my best friend, so I could tell her anything, right?

"Monet—" I hesitated.

"What?"

"I wanted to ask you something about Dev," I said hesitantly.

"Sophie Donnelly, don't you dare go there," she said hotly. "My brother is not some arm candy you can use for your own purposes and then toss aside."

"I didn't say—"

"You didn't have to," she replied. "I know how your scheming little mind works. Did you ever ask yourself why I put up with you for so long?"

"I didn't realize you were *putting up* with me," I said. "I thought we were best friends."

She hesitated. "You know I didn't mean it like that."

"How did you mean it?"

"It's just—I always knew that you were so into Connor and being popular that you'd never look in Dev's direction."

"Don't you trust me?" I said. I was getting a little angry myself. She was supposed to be my best friend.

"Now that you mention it, I don't," she said. "At least not with Dev's fragile little heart. Let me be perfectly clear. I do not want you going near Dev. You'll just ruin him for anybody else and then dump him when somebody new comes along."

"But what if I —"

"What?" she snapped. "What could you possibly say to convince me?"

"Never mind." I chickened out and hung up without telling her the truth, which turned out to be a seriously bad judgment call.

# Chapter 19

The next day, I jumped at every shadow. As I walked down the hall, I felt like everyone was staring at me. Guilt colored every movement. I flinched every time I passed Olivia in the hall, but she just gave me a Cheshire cat grin and kept on going.

By sixth period, I was almost hoping that it would happen, just to get it over with. If nothing else, the experience taught me that I didn't have the steely nerves of a successful criminal.

Then I saw Haley and Vanessa in the hallway. As they breezed by me, Vanessa said, "So, Dev Lucero, huh? Nice."

The news was out. Olivia's jaw must have hurt from all the talking she'd done.

It wasn't completely unheard of for her to text message a juicy bit of dirt, but she usually preferred to deliver the news in person. That way she had the satisfaction of seeing everyone's reaction.

And people evidently couldn't resist embellishing the truth. So I wasn't surprised that everyone was buzzing, but I was surprised to hear the following versions of the rumor:

a) Dev and I had been meeting in secret for months. He was the real reason Connor and I had broken up.

b) Connor, Dev, and I were currently in the midst of a steamy love triangle, and Connor was on the verge of breaking up with Angie for me.

c) Dev and Connor had fought over me.

d) Dev was so jealous that he'd given Connor a black eye.

Connor had a black eye, but it was because of an enthusiastic game of racquetball. Chase's elbow accidentally making contact with Connor's eye was the cause, not Dev's fist.

But, of course, Olivia couldn't wait to spread the news. What I didn't expect was for Monet to confront her about it and call her a liar.

They faced off in the hallway.

"You know, Olivia, you've always had a big mouth, but I never thought you were a liar. A gossip, yes, but not a liar."

"I'm not a liar," Olivia said. "Am I, Sophie?"

I blushed.

"This time you've gone too far," Monet said.

"Monet—"

"No, Sophie, let me finish." She held up a hand to silence me. "Olivia, Sophie is my best friend. She would never betray my trust by hooking up with my brother and not telling me. Right, Sophie?"

I *was* a terrible liar, which was ironic, since it was almost a popularity prerequisite. Acting wasn't lying, it was becoming someone else, so I tried to think of myself as a wrongly accused innocent, but it wasn't working.

"Sophie?" Monet repeated my name, but the betrayal she felt was written on her face.

"Monet, I . . . it just happened."

My explanation was lost on her as she marched off without a backward glance.

"I hope you're happy," I turned to Olivia.

"Ecstatic," she said. She smiled cattily at me. "What's the problem, anyway? Monet will get over it. Dev's hot, and you two will be the most popular couple in school."

I replied without thinking, "We're not a couple."

Her smile grew wider. "Oh, really?"

"Not yet," I amended quickly. "It's just so new." The last thing I wanted was a rumor that I hooked up indiscriminately. Unfortunately, the double standard was alive and well at Kennedy High.

Olivia fairly vibrated with excitement, and I

cursed my wild tongue. But I couldn't take it back without looking like an even bigger fool. And if I did tell her the truth, who knew what rumors she'd spread?

I couldn't bear it if Connor or Angie heard that I was pining for Connor, especially since I wasn't even sure I was pining. But I was sure I was confused.

Olivia scurried off and I knew that I had made a big mistake. Again.

It was raining, so we were confined to the cafeteria. My mood was darker than the cloudy sky. Monet still wasn't talking to me.

I surveyed the room, gripping my tray. Where was I supposed to sit? Monet wasn't in the caf. She was probably holed up in the art room with Scott. Maybe even making a little voodoo doll of me. The girl had skills.

Vanessa and Haley waved to me. "Sophie, over here."

They were sharing a table with a couple of girls from drama, but from the way Haley had her back to them, she made it clear she wasn't sitting with them. I sat between them, in the no-man's-land between popular and forgettable.

"Hi, Sophie," Ava said.

Haley nudged me, then deliberately turned her back. I was tired of talking only to the popular people.

"Hi," I said. "Hey, did you have fun at that concert?"

"I can't believe you missed it," Ava said. "Next time you should go with us."

I smiled at her. "Maybe I will. Let me know."

Haley nudged me again, but I ignored her. I wasn't going to let her tell me who I could talk to. I was so over that. Why did she care who I talked to, anyway? Did popularity have to mean I acted like a snob?

Dev stomped up and grabbed my arm. "I need to talk to you. Alone."

"Well, hello to you, too," Haley said with a pout.

Dev ignored her and steered me into the empty hallway. "I want you to stop those rumors about us," he said.

"Yanking me out of the caf wasn't exactly the best way to go about it," I said mildly.

"I don't have time for your crap today," he said. "Monet is acting like I peed in her cornflakes or something. And all everyone is talking about is —"

"Is us," I finished for him.

"Yes," he said furiously. "God, are you so concerned about being popular that you had to spread that rumor?"

Ice settled in my stomach. I opened my mouth to deny it, but then I snapped it closed as just as quickly. Why did Dev always think the worst of me?

"How do I know that *you* didn't start that rumor?" I asked him.

"Get over yourself, Sophie Donnelly," he said. "I would never tell anyone that I'd kissed you. I'm ashamed of myself."

"Then why did you kiss me?" I practically shouted.

"Keep your voice down," Dev said. "Or is that part of your plan?"

"Now who needs to get over himself? You didn't answer the question. Why did you kiss me if I'm so repulsive?"

"I — I felt sorry for you," he said.

"You felt sorry for me?" I said. Fury surged through my veins. Was he trying to humiliate me even more than I already was? "Well, don't. There are plenty of guys who want to kiss me."

"Only the stupid ones, like Tanner," he hissed. "Or the desperate ones, like Jason Brady."

I froze. "I think you've said enough."

I went back to the caf. That's what Dev really thought of me? That you had to be stupid or desperate to kiss me?

Was that what everyone else thought? No wonder I wasn't popular any longer.

"Sophie, have you seen this?" Ava waved her phone in front of me.

"What is it?"

"It's the latest hotness poll," she replied.

"So?" I said indifferently.

"You don't seem very excited about it," she said. She pointed to something on the screen.

"What are you talking about?"

"You're number one, baby," she said.

"What? That can't be right." I grabbed the phone from her hands.

I stared at the words in front of me. Apparently, I had regained my hotness. And it didn't take a boyfriend or trashing another girl to do it. Who knew? And now that I was back on top, I was surprised to find I didn't even care.

"Are you okay?" Ava said.

"I'm fine," I said. "Just surprised. Thanks for telling me." I handed the phone back to her.

"What was that all about, with you and Dev? He seemed angry about something."

I found myself telling her the whole pathetic story. "And the worst part is that Monet is furious with me."

"Do you like her brother?"

"I don't know. Sometimes I think I hate him," I replied honestly. "But I'm not sure if he likes me."

"Oh, you have it bad."

I was very afraid Ava was right.

# Chapter 20

Ava took pity on me in my friendless state. "Want to go see a movie this weekend?" she asked.

"Are you sure you want to be seen with me?"

"I think I can take the heat," she replied.

"Cool."

We went to see the latest blockbuster. It wasn't really Ava's cup of tea, but I think she suggested it in the hopes of cheering me up. I avoided the Good & Plenty and opted for the more substantial nachos.

"Nothing like a cheesy flick to make me feel better," I said, propping my feet up on the row in front of me.

"Can't I take you anywhere?" she said. "That," she pointed to my feet, "is just rude. Somebody's head is gonna be there in a few minutes. Would you want your hair up against someone's feet?"

She was right. I put my feet down. "Sorry."

"No worries," she said. "Now, hand over some of those nachos."

We'd gotten there early because Ava insisted on getting seats in the back row.

"I forgot to get a soda," I said. "I'm heading to the snack bar. You want anything?"

"No, thanks," she replied.

There was a long line at the snack bar, so I decided to hit the restroom before the movie started. When I walked in, I saw Olivia Kaplan fixing her makeup at the mirror and then heard a familiar voice emanating from one of the stalls.

"Can you believe she's here with that fat lesbo? And to think Sophie used to be popular. But I fixed her." A little chuckle followed.

Olivia's eyes met mine in the mirror. She opened her mouth to say something, but I shook my head and she froze.

"Is that Haley Owens's voice I hear?"

Silence. Then, "Sophie, I didn't know you were here. I'll be right out."

She emerged from the stall and rushed to give me a hug. I sidestepped her. "I interrupted you in the middle of a story. Please go on."

"I — I — I was just joking," she stuttered. "I knew you were there all along."

"Haley, I know it was you who took that photo of me at the dance," I said. "And I was prepared to forgive you, but don't talk trash about my friends." I leaned in closer and said softly, so that only she could hear, "And if I ever hear that you called Ava names again, I'll personally see to it that a few photos of *you* are passed around."

A little louder, I said, "Good, I'm glad we understand each other. Have a nice day." Score one for my big mouth!

I swept from the room, leaving Olivia and Haley gaping. They deserved each other. How could I have been stupid enough to think Haley was my friend? Olivia was bad, spreading malicious gossip, but she was open about it. Haley was worst of all, pretending to be my friend while stabbing me in the back.

"You were gone a long time," Ava observed when I returned.

I handed her a pack of gummi bears. She loved gummi bears. "Here."

"What are these for?"

"They're a thank-you," I said, "for being a good friend."

Just then, Dev and Beth walked in. I ducked down in my seat. "Oh, no."

"What is it?"

I motioned to where they stood, scanning the theater to find seats. It was crowded, but there were seats next to us.

"Do you want to leave?" Ava said.

"No, of course not," I said.

But she wasn't convinced. "Let's get out of here," she said. "We can watch the movie in the next theater. C'mon, before they see us."

But it was too late. "Hi, Ava. Hi, Sophie. Do you mind if we sit here?" Beth asked.

What could I say? "Of course not."

It was almost worth my own discomfort when I saw Dev's expression.

"I'll get us some snacks," he said. He practically bolted down the aisle, as if fleeing the scene of a crime.

Beth chatted away, completely oblivious to my discomfort.

Ava shot me a puzzled look, but I shook my head. Beth wasn't doing it on purpose, at least I didn't think she was. She wasn't aware of the gossip about Dev and me because she was too much of a straight edge to listen to it.

When Dev got back, the only seat left was the one next to me. He sat there because he didn't have any other choice, but I could tell he'd rather be anywhere else.

Thankfully, the movie started, which discouraged any conversation. Beth, I noticed, talked during movies.

I kept my eyes on the screen but was hyperaware of Dev's every move. I swore I would kill him if he made a move on Beth in front of me, but he kept his hands firmly on his own side of the armrest.

Still, I was consumed with jealousy.

His leg bumped against mine once and he whispered a "sorry," but other than that, we didn't exchange one single word.

It was the longest hour and a half of my life. When the lights went up, I practically bolted down the aisle.

Outside, Ava looked at me. "So, how did you like the movie?" she said deadpan, but I could see the twinkle in her eye.

"That wasn't funny," I said, "it was horrible. You have the worst taste in movies."

We burst into hysterical laughter.

# Chapter 21

"No, no, no," Mr. Fanelli shouted. "Try it again. And, Dev, this time, kiss her like you mean it, not like you're kissing your grandmother." We were practicing the wedding scene and Fanelli had it in his head that we needed a big kiss at the end.

"Can't we just stage kiss? The audience can't even tell the difference, anyway," I pleaded. I mean, how embarrassing. Dev wasn't even trying to hide his reluctance to put his lips on mine.

"*I* can tell," Mr. Fanelli replied, "so no, you can't. We are striving for authenticity, Sophie. We want the audience to think that you and Dev are passionately in love, carried away, transported."

"Let's just get this over with," I said to Dev. He grunted, which was what passed for communication from him these days.

He put his arms around me, but it looked

artificial, even to me. There was no feeling in his arms or his lips. I kept my own lips firmly closed.

Mr. Fanelli clapped his hands again. "Wait, wait," he said. "This is not working. We need fire." He snapped his fingers. "Angie, Connor, come show Sophie and Dev how it's done."

"Great," I whispered furiously to Dev, "now we have to take kissing lessons from Connor."

"Not if I can help it," Dev said. He grabbed me and planted a long, slow kiss on my lips. He moved to the curve of my cheek and murmured, "Kiss me back, Sophie."

So I did. Wildly. Gladly. Passionately. I forgot about our audience, forgot that I was angry with him, and forgot everything except the feeling of him pressed against me.

The sound of applause brought me to my senses, and I ended the kiss. The cast finally went back to what they were doing, Connor frowned, and Dev disappeared, but I still stood there.

Monet bustled up with the pretense of showing me something. "Don't stand there like a guppy with your mouth open, Sophie."

They were the first words she'd spoken to me in days. "We were just acting," I said quickly.

"I get it now," she said.

"Get what?" But she ignored me and went back to her clipboard.

When Mr. Fanelli called a five-minute break, I decided to pass out the cookies I'd made the night before.

"Can I talk to you?"

It was Connor. I handed him a chocolate chip cookie and then remembered that they were his favorite. So what? I told myself, they were everybody's favorite.

Connor led me to a corner of the auditorium, but I balked. "I'm not having an audience to our conversation. Not again. Whatever you have to say to me, you need to say it in private."

"Okay, that's fair. Hallway okay?"

I poked my head out the door and surveyed the hallway. Deserted. "Make it quick."

He followed me out. "I wanted to say something," he began. He gave me his trademark roguish grin, the one he used to charm me into going out with him in the first place. If I knew my ex-boyfriend, he was about to ask me for a favor.

"You may have heard that Angie and I have been having some problems lately."

"I never listen to idle gossip," I replied. Hey, if you can't lie to an ex-boyfriend, who can you lie to?

"It's just not working out. I was so stupid before, the way I treated you. And you're so great. . . ."

Oh, no. It couldn't be. Dread filled my stomach. Connor couldn't be asking me out again, could he? As he spoke, I realized that I was completely and utterly over him. I wouldn't take him back even if it meant that I would never be popular again.

"Connor, listen, you're great, too, but I'm not into you anymore."

He looked startled. "I know that."

"You do?"

"Yes, but I thought maybe you could talk to Angie. Let her know that I'm a great catch. That kind of thing. I think she might be losing interest."

Was it possible that Connor was actually unsure of himself? He was, probably for the first time ever.

"I don't know," I replied. "Can I ask you a question?"

"Anything." He smiled charmingly.

"Tell me why you dumped me in the first place." Monet said I never learned, but maybe I could learn from this.

"I don't know why," he said.

"Of course you do," I replied. "You're just afraid that if you tell me, I'll get mad and do something stupid."

"Won't you?"

I winced. "Probably," I admitted. "But I'm trying not to."

He shrugged. "Remember when we met? You were kind of awkward and a little shy. I thought you needed me. But after a while, it seemed like the only thing you needed was to be talked about, no matter how you went about doing it."

"You liked me because I needed rescuing?"

"Everyone needs to be needed," he said. "I did care about you, but it started to feel like you didn't really care about me. Angie did."

I didn't say anything. I stood there trying to absorb what he was saying.

"That's it? No scenes, no drama?"

"Nope."

He grinned. "Why, Sophie, I believe you must be changing."

"So what exactly do you want me to do?" I wasn't going to completely transform, at least not overnight, anyhow. These things take time.

"I want you to convince Angie that there are no hard feelings."

"Why does she care?"

"She thinks it was bad for her image, the way I broke up with you. She wants us to hang out to show everyone that everything's okay."

Translation: She was worried that everyone thought she was a boyfriend-stealing ho.

"Why should I do this for you?" Or for Angie, for that matter. But maybe it would give me some sort of closure. It took a lot of energy to hate someone.

"Why? You have firsthand experience. I was a good boyfriend to you, and I'd be a good friend." He said it with such confidence that I didn't have the heart to point out that good boyfriends don't dump their girlfriends in public.

"I'll try, Connor, but I can't make any promises."

"Let's meet at Wicked Jack's later tonight."

"Tonight?" It wasn't like I had anything better to do.

"Please?" he said.

"Angie has to come, too." The last thing I needed was new rumors about Connor and me getting back together or something ridiculous like that.

"Then you'll do it? Sophie, I love you!" He picked me up and whirled me around.

"Put me down," I said, but I was laughing as I said it. Connor's exuberance was contagious.

"Not until you say yes."

"Yes, yes. I'll meet you tonight. Now put me down before someone sees us."

But someone already had. Dev was glowering at us from the doorway of the auditorium. "They need us," he said curtly.

Connor set me down, and we followed Dev back into rehearsal. Connor wandered off and I was left to deal with Dev.

"What's your problem?" I said, but he didn't answer.

We went through another scene, thankfully not one in which we were supposed to kiss.

Mr. Fanelli called out, "Okay, people. Let's call it a night. Dress rehearsal on Thursday. Don't be late."

Connor and I left together and waited for Angie by his car. We were heading to the restaurant as soon as she managed to tear herself away from whatever it was that she was doing. The waiting was irritating me and I looked at my watch again.

"You can ride with us, you know," Connor said.

"Now you're pushing it," I said.

Dev walked by us.

"Good night, Dev," I called out, but he ignored me and got into his car. A minute later, it tore out of the parking lot.

"What's with him?" Connor said. But the subject was dropped when he saw Angie.

"Let's get this over with," she said.

"Hey, I'm the one doing you two a favor," I said. "I'm not the one who broke up a happy couple."

She observed me for a long minute. "You have a point," she said. "But let's call it a mutually beneficial endeavor."

I hated it, but she thought like me. And she was right. Monet still wasn't talking to me, and I needed all the friendly encounters I could get.

# Chapter 22

The dinner with my former boyfriend and my archrival was a success. The rumor mill had done its job and spread the word of our amicable outing at Wicked Jack's.

I had convinced everyone that Connor and I were buddies again. And there was a bonus, because after watching him fawn all over Angie, I realized that I no longer had any feelings for him. But I did feel something for Dev.

As soon as I was done with my classes, I was going to go tell Dev how I felt about him.

But first, my best friend.

"Can I talk to you?" I waited at Monet's locker again, just like I had for the past week, but she clearly wouldn't even look at me. She slammed her locker shut and walked off.

I trailed after her, determined to apologize fully, even though she clearly didn't want to hear it.

"I'm sorry I didn't tell you what happened between Dev and me," I continued.

Olivia Kaplan made a beeline for us, elbowing a couple of people out of her way to get to the scoop. I wasn't going to let her stop me. If she wanted to tell everyone what I said to Monet, let her. It was more important that I salvage my friendship.

Monet increased her pace, but I persisted. "I didn't tell you because I knew you would be mad. I didn't plan it, I swear. And I definitely didn't do it just to become popular again, no matter what your brother thinks or what rumors are floating around."

She stopped. "Why should I believe you?"

"Have I ever lied to you before?"

She shook her head.

"Monet, honestly, I'm sorry. It won't happen again."

She gave me a level stare. "Are you telling me that you're not attracted to my brother?"

It was a test, I knew. I had to decide which was more important, my pride or my best friend. It was an easy decision.

"I am attracted to Dev," I admitted.

"I knew it!"

"But I didn't realize it, not until he kissed me."

Olivia soaked up every word. Monet turned to her. "Don't you have something better to do?"

"Not really," she replied.

"Really?" Monet said. She smirked at her. "Because I hear you have some*one* better to do. So you'd better scamper unless you want the whole school to hear, too."

Olivia took off like a bolt of lightning.

I looked at Monet in awe. "What was that all about?"

"Let's just say that Olivia just confirmed a suspicion and leave it at that," she answered. "Now, about my brother —"

"It's over. I promise."

For the rest of the day, I was so happy to be friends with Monet again, I smiled at everyone I met. And they smiled back.

"You're awfully chipper," Monet commented.

"I know," I said.

We exchanged grins.

"Hey, Hannah, I love that top." I beamed at her. "Quincy, nice article in the paper."

I ignored the "What's up with her?" and the "Is she running for Homecoming queen or something?" and even the bewildered "But she never talks to me."

At lunch, we were back at our usual table, only now, Scott and Ava and a couple of Ava's friends joined us.

"Whew," Ava said. "I'm glad you two finally made up."

"Me, too," I said. "Although it was nice hanging out with you. I'm afraid now you're stuck with me. With us, really, because Monet and I are a team."

Monet reached over and squeezed my hand hard, which meant that I was truly forgiven, but also meant "Don't you dare start any of your crap."

"While you two were fighting," Ava confided to Monet, "the girl was so miserable, I could barely stand to be around her."

We all laughed, but it was true. I'd learned my lesson, and if it meant I had to give up Dev to keep Monet's friendship, then I'd do it.

"So what's the current status of the Dev and Sophie saga?" Ava said.

I shot a quick glance at Monet. Her face was expressionless.

"Uh, maybe we should talk about something else?"

"It's okay," Monet said. "But, everyone, please remember, he is my brother, so please, no gory details."

"There aren't any gory details," I protested.

Monet raised an eyebrow.

"Sophie's blushing!" Ava crowed.

"Cut it out, you guys," I said. "Dev's not even talking to me right now. And besides, I promised Monet nothing else will happen."

She smiled at me. "Actually, I hereby give you permission to date Dev. With the caveat that you don't become one of those annoying couples who are all starry-eyed all the time."

"You mean, like you and Scott?" I said.

Now it was her turn to blush.

The lunch bell rang.

"Saved by the bell," Ava said.

I linked arms with her and Monet. "Did I ever tell you that *Saved by the Bell* was Monet's favorite television show when we were little?"

"It was not," Monet said. She squirmed when we giggled.

"It was, too," I said. "You had the maddest crush on Screech."

Ava erupted into laughter. "That explains so much," she said.

"How did the ex dinner go?" Monet asked.

"You're not going to believe it," I said.

"Try me."

"Angie wanted to bury the hatchet."

"My brother seems to be under the impression that you and Connor are back together."

"Why would he think that?" I said, then remembered the scene in the hallway. I stopped walking. "Oh, no."

I explained to her what happened. "What am I going to do?"

"Tell him the truth."

"But I don't even know if he likes me," I replied.

"He'll be getting in a couple of laps at the school pool before rehearsal," she said. "Go find him then."

So after my last class, I went in search of Dev. I was glad that I had talked to Connor. I didn't need him in order to be happy. In fact, to tell the truth, I'd been much happier without him. Only my pride had been hurt, not my heart.

At first, I thought the pool was deserted. There wasn't anyone in the water. Then I noticed Dev, sitting at the edge at the far end. But he wasn't alone. He was with Angie, talking and laughing.

I swallowed back the anger and turned on my heels and went home. It was all her fault, I told myself over and over on the drive home. She'd stolen Connor, and now she was trying to take Dev, too. It was the last straw. The war was back on.

# Chapter 23

I couldn't get the image of the two of them out of my mind. It seared my brain as I threw my backpack down in our hallway and stomped to the kitchen. It was about a hundred times more painful than when Connor dumped me.

I stood in front of the cupboard and surveyed my mother's spices.

I'd read something about a beauty contest being sabotaged when someone put chili powder or something in the contestant's clothing. It had made her itch and sneeze, and I was hoping to find something to do the same to Angie.

"Honey, are you home?" Mom hollered from the front door. "I need help with the groceries."

"Coming, Mom," I yelled back, but I didn't move.

I hesitated, hand in the air, but then the image of Dev smiling at Angie flashed into my mind, and

I grabbed the cayenne pepper and put it in my backpack.

I told myself that it didn't have anything to do with the fact that I'd seen her flirting with Dev. It was about the play.

Still, as I helped Mom with the groceries, the hurt feeling wouldn't go away. It was much worse than when Connor had betrayed me. I didn't think Dev would be fooled by a pair of pouty lips and fake eyelashes, but apparently, he was as weak as all the rest.

I was going to put my plan into motion at school the next day. I cut my last class and snuck into the costume closet. The lighting was dim in there and the room felt unbearably stuffy.

Angie's outfit was hanging right in front. It was almost too easy. I started to sweat but managed to turn her costume inside out. I whipped out the spice jar and sprinkled the powder all over her gown.

The dismissal bell rang and I threw the jar into my backpack and slipped out before classes emptied out into the hall.

A few minutes later, I strolled into rehearsal. Monet and Fanelli were the only ones in the room.

"What's with you?" Monet said. "You're never here on time."

"I cut class," I said, without thinking. Mr. Fanelli gave me a dirty look and I added quickly, "I wanted to go somewhere quiet and prepare."

His frown faded, but he still had to give me a lecture. "Sophie, I don't approve of skipping classes."

"I won't do it again," I promised rashly.

My answer seemed to satisfy him, because he only grunted and went back to his clipboard.

Monet said, "We have a couple of minutes before we start. Want to get a soda?"

Perfect. An alibi.

We headed to the vending machine outside.

"I'm really proud of you, you know," she said.

"Why is that?"

"Because you kept your promise," she said.

"What promise?"

She gave me a friendly sock on the arm. "Quit kidding around."

I had a feeling I was heading for trouble, so for once I decided to think before I spoke. "Oh, that."

While she continued to talk, I frantically tried to recall what she could be talking about. The promise not to regain my social status by any means necessary — like costume sabotage?

I started to sweat. If she found out what I'd done, she'd never forgive me, as a stage manager or a friend.

"We should get back to rehearsal," I reminded her.

We hurried back into the auditorium, where most of the cast were gathered.

Monet said, "C'mon, people, time to get into costume and makeup."

The drama classroom had been converted. The desks were gone and several rows of temporary makeup chairs had been set up in their places.

One of Monet's lackeys wheeled a clothing rack filled with our costumes into the room. I changed into my dress and threw a robe over it to protect the fabric when I was in hair and makeup. My costume was the typical ingenue white, pretty but boring.

Mrs. Swenson, who volunteered for every production even after her daughter had graduated, waved me over. I liked her the best of all the volunteer moms and gladly went into her chair.

"Sophie, how are you? You'll dazzle us tonight, I'm sure."

"Thanks, Mrs. Swenson. I hope so," I replied. "How is Shelli?"

We chatted about her daughter's college experience while Mrs. Swenson braided my hair and twisted it into a bun in the back of my head. Then she applied thick greasepaint to my face and finished the rest of my makeup.

Finally, I was ready. I thanked her and hopped out of the chair, giving up my place to Vanessa, who was playing a minor role as a widow.

Fanelli hollered, "Places, everyone!" The words

gave me that familiar thrill. I'd been so focused on climbing back to the top that I'd forgotten how to enjoy the acting process.

Angie sneezed once backstage. A little flurry of spice rose from her dress. I looked around, but no one else noticed. I thought everything was going according to plan.

It was my chance. I'd have the role I'd always wanted, the role of tempestuous Katharina, the role I thought I was meant to play.

"Do you smell cayenne pepper?" she said.

Mr. Fanelli didn't even yell at her for breaking character. "Angie, are you feeling okay?"

A little panicky feeling fluttered in my chest. She didn't look well. Her eyes were all red and her face was starting to swell.

"Cayenne?" Connor said, his voice rising. "You're allergic to cayenne pepper."

"I know," she said, her speech thickening.

She was having an allergic reaction.

"Does anyone have any Benadryl?" Monet asked.

"Get her some water," Fanelli shouted.

"I think I have some Benadryl in my purse," I said. There was a sick feeling in my stomach. I didn't like Angie, but I didn't wish her any real harm.

I ran backstage and grabbed my backpack. I rummaged through it until I found the over-the-counter medicine I was looking for and returned to the stage.

Angie chugged a huge bottle of water, sitting on a chair surrounded by the cast and crew. I was relieved to see that the swelling in her face was already receding.

"Here you go," I said. I handed it to Connor, and that's when I noticed the reddish-brown powder all over my hand. I looked down. There was a trail of pepper running down the skirt of my white dress. I tried to hide my hand, but it was too late.

"What's that all over your skirt?" Monet said.

Everyone was staring at me.

"It's cayenne pepper," Dev said. The disappointment in his voice nearly made me cry.

"It's not," I said. "It's . . . from lunch."

I tried to hand Connor the Benadryl, but he refused it. "Like I'd take anything from you," he said. "It's already taken care of. She had an EpiPen in her bag."

Monet grabbed my backpack and shook out the contents.

"Hey!" I said, but it was too late.

She dug into it until she found something. "Aha," she said. She held up a small container. "*This* is cayenne papper."

There were general expressions of disgust from the crowd, but I ignored them. I only cared about Monet at that point. "It was just a p-prank."

Monet gave a snort of disbelief.

"I didn't know she was allergic," I said pleadingly, but Monet was stone-faced.

"Don't ever talk to me again," she said.

Fanelli, for once, hadn't commented until then. "Monet, take over the dress rehearsal. Vanessa will stand in as Bianca. Sophie, in my office. Now."

# Chapter 24

I didn't even try the drama queen act.

Fanelli yelled at me for about twenty minutes and I sat there, taking it, without saying a word. He was right, after all.

"I honestly didn't know she was allergic," I finally said, when he ran out of steam. "I just wanted the role of Katharina so badly, I didn't think."

He sighed. "I can't tell you how disappointed I am. You're lucky she wasn't seriously hurt."

"I would never deliberately try to hurt her," I said. "I just wanted to make her sneeze so much that she'd blow the dress rehearsal and you'd give me that role."

"That was never going to happen," he said.

"I know that now," I said. "And I'm truly sorry."

It was a miracle, but Fanelli took pity on me. I would still be allowed to play Bianca, but I was banned from participating in the spring musical, and I had to help with cleanup for every drama event in the near future. I got off lightly.

I went home before the dress rehearsal was over. I left my costume hanging on the empty rack. I'd managed to brush most of the pepper from it.

Mom was home and I threw myself down on the couch, crying, as I told her everything.

"Oh, honey," she said. "It's just high school. You make mistakes and you move on."

"Everyone sees me the way they want to see me," I said. "Monet wants to see me as this nice girl, Connor wanted to see me as someone to rescue, and Dev doesn't want to see me at all."

"You *are* a nice girl," my mom said.

"But that's not all I am. And I'm not just a drama queen, either. Why does she expect me to always be nice? Or why do other people expect me to be mean? Why can't I be some of those things some of the time?"

"You can be," she said. "But no matter what you do, try to be a better you."

It sounded like a public relations slogan, but it wasn't bad advice.

"I can try," I said. I gave her a hug. "Thanks, Mom. I'm heading to bed."

I wanted to stay there, preferably until I was thirty, but I had to get up and face the hostility. I didn't dare check my DramaDivas page to see what people were saying about me. Still, I wasn't prepared for the viciousness of the rumors when I went to school the next day. It was Friday, and that night was opening night.

"I heard she tried to kill Angie Vogel," someone said as I stood in the lunch line at the caf. There was no sign of Monet or Dev, but I knew they wouldn't talk to me even if they'd been in the cafeteria.

I couldn't face it. I grabbed an apple and some juice and decided to hole up in the library and run my lines. I couldn't blow that, too.

Finally, it was an hour before curtain time, which meant the usual complete chaos. Monet was in a state of high anxiety, and I didn't even dare look at Dev. I didn't want to push my luck. Besides, everyone was still avoiding me.

"I can't find my costume," Angie shrieked.

Monet threw a poisonous look my way and I gave her a tiny shake of my head. I'd learned my lesson.

"Oh, my God. I'm going to throw up," Angie shrieked. She sounded mere minutes from unraveling. A little part of me reveled in her breakdown.

But I didn't want it anymore, at least not like that. Even if it did mean she was distracted from being mad at me.

"You'll be fine," I said. "Take deep breaths. Everyone is nervous opening night."

Monet gave me a tiny smile when she thought I wasn't looking.

"Just pretend everyone in the audience is naked," I suggested.

Angie let out a wail. "My parents will be in the audience!"

"Then no," I said. "Pretend that there's no one there."

"Is that what you do to forget about all those people?" Angie asked. "You seem so calm."

I was calm as long as I ignored the time bomb lodged in my stomach. I didn't tell her my pre-show ritual of biting my nails down to the quick. I'd already booked a manicure as soon as the show ended.

"Just look into — into Connor's eyes," I said. I was proud that I only stumbled over the words the tiniest bit. "Forget about everyone else. Just focus on how much he cares about you."

I saw a couple of the kids whispering and snickering, and I squared my chin. Let them talk. They were wrong about me, whatever they were saying.

"Thanks, Sophie," Angie said. "That's good advice."

"Two minutes to curtain," Monet said. And I felt my stomach drop to my knees. I tried to remember my own advice and forget about everything, but a lot was riding on this.

If I screwed up and ruined the opening night performance, Monet would never believe I hadn't done it deliberately. But chances were good that opening night would go smoothly. Dress rehearsal certainly hadn't, and it was a stage tradition that if you had a bad dress rehearsal, it meant a great opening night.

The curtain went up and we took our places. I could barely hear my cue over the hammering of my heart.

It all started going downhill during the first scene, when Angie stumbled over her opening line. "I —" (long pause) "I pray . . ." Her face went white.

*"You, sir,"* I gave her a prompt without moving my lips.

"You, sir, is it your will to make a stale of me amongst these mates?" she continued.

I released a breath I didn't even know I'd been holding and got ready for my cue. I let myself be transported to another time and place, into another person, a person who was as pliable as a willow tree.

Then it was time for my exit. Angie was supposed to exit a few lines later and I held my breath, but she remembered her lines and exited when she was supposed to.

She rushed up to me. "Oh, my God. I can't believe you did that!"

Monet's head whipped around. "What did she do now?" she said in a weary tone.

"She saved my ass," Angie said. "I went blank and she fed me the line."

I noticed that Dev was eavesdropping on the whole conversation, but when I glanced at him, he looked away. My scene had been going surprisingly well, but the big kiss was yet to come.

"Really?" Monet said.

"Don't sound so surprised," I said.

Monet opened her mouth, but then Guy Squires rushed up. "There's a problem with the sound board," he said, and she took off to deal with the minor emergency.

Angie stumbled a couple more times. "I don't know what's wrong with me," she said during intermission.

A couple of things sprang to mind, but I bit my tongue. Till I drew blood. At this rate, the turning-over-a-new-leaf thing was going to be even more painful than I had anticipated.

"Relax," I said. "You're doing fine."

But she really blew it during the wedding scene. Connor said something and then her face went white. Her mouth moved, but nothing came out.

She looked at him pleadingly, but Connor could barely remember his own lines. He couldn't come to the rescue this time.

He just stood there waiting. Finally, he repeated her cue again.

My mind went blank, too, for a second and then the words came back to me. I bent down and pretended to adjust the train of Angie's gown and whispered the words to her.

Her face relaxed and she projected loud and clear.

The curtain finally went down and we took our bows. I breathed a sigh of relief. It was over for the night.

"What was all that about?" Dev said.

"Oh, so you're talking to me now?" I replied.

"What was going on?"

"None of your business." When we kissed during the wedding scene, he had given me a kiss that had thrilled me to my toes, and I thought he might have forgiven me, but I guess I was wrong. He had just been acting.

How could he have missed that Angie had frozen?

"Sophie, why can't you just leave her alone?"

"Why can't you?" I said, before stomping off. I took a certain amount of glee in the surprise I saw on his face. I was reforming, but there was no way I was going to let Dev Lucero boss me around.

I only had two more performances to get through. Saturday afternoon, we were already in costume when Monet came up to me.

"That was nice of you, what you did for Angie last night."

"It was the least I could do after I tried to kill her," I said. It was a weak attempt at a joke, but Monet didn't laugh and I couldn't blame her.

"Do you want to hang out at the cast party?" she said after an awkward pause.

I met her eyes. "I'm trying to change," I said. "But I can't guarantee that I'll always be a perfect angel."

She suppressed a snort. "Of that I have no doubt." And that's when I knew I was forgiven.

I gave her a hug and noticed Dev watching us. All I saw in his eyes was contempt, but I couldn't live with myself if I didn't at least try to tell him how I felt.

Before I had time to talk to him and pour out my heart, however, we were called into hair and makeup. I'd corner him at the cast party, I decided.

Vanessa's mom used to be a professional makeup artist and had volunteered to help do makeup for the play. I changed into a robe and then took my place in front of one of the lighted mirrors that had been temporarily added to the girls' locker room.

While Mrs. Leon applied the thick stage paint to my face, I sat in the chair and mentally ran my lines one more time.

A few minutes later, there was a knock at the door and Haley, who wasn't changing into costume or at the makeup table, answered it. She came back with a bouquet of flowers.

"They're for you," she said, handing me an enormous spray of orchids.

"Who would send me flowers?" I said.

"Probably your mom," Haley said.

I gave her a dirty look, but she smiled sweetly.

"There's a card," she added helpfully.

I opened the envelope. The card said "Break a leg. Dev."

I wondered if he meant that literally.

# Chapter 25

"Every seat in the house is full," Monet whispered to me. "It's a sold-out performance."

"Did Fanelli promise them they could throw rotten tomatoes at me?" I whispered back. I always made jokes when I was nervous. I was trying not to let it show, but my hands were clammy with sweat. Opening night is always a blur; now this felt *real.*

"No, but maybe rumors of your torrid love affair with my brother drew a crowd," Monet shot back.

I paled.

"Hey, it's okay," she said. "I was just joking."

It killed me to admit it, but Connor and Angie did a good job. She made an admirable Katharina, blowing hot one minute and cold the next. It was a better than decent performance, but I knew my Katharina would have been something special. There was bound to be a college production, if I was lucky.

I heard my cue and stepped into the scene. I said my first line and Dev replied. My shoulders were incredibly tense, but after a few minutes, I felt them loosen.

I could do this. As I said the words, it finally became clear. I was a girl in love with a guy.

When Dev took me into his arms, I thought, despite Fanelli's directions, he might try to fake it with a stage kiss. Instead, he took me into his arms and kissed me lingeringly.

I vaguely heard the sound of a wolf whistle from the audience. I was so addled that I could barely get out my next line, but I managed.

Monet later told me that the look of dazed lust on my face lent my performance a little extra something. I didn't point out that I hadn't been acting.

I said my last line, "The more fool you, for laying on my duty." I almost tripped as I exited the stage, but I caught myself and hoped nobody noticed.

When the curtain finally fell, there was a moment of silence and then the crowd burst into roaring applause. *Everyone* was clapping, even the kids who buy tickets to the shows just to make fun of them.

Backstage, everyone was talking and laughing at once. Even Dev looked my way and smiled.

"Go on and take your bow," Mr. Fanelli said to me. "You've earned it."

The leads linked hands and went forward to take their bows. Dev was on one side of me and Connor was on the other, but I barely noticed him. I was reveling in the sensation of Dev's hand in mine.

A strange exhilaration mixed with sadness came over me as we took our final bow. And finally, the last of the applause for Mr. Fanelli and Monet as they came out and took theirs. Then the houselights went up and the audience filed out.

I found Mom, who handed me a bouquet of white roses. "From your father," she said. "He's sorry he couldn't make it. And this," Mom said, giving me a hug, "is from me."

"Best present ever," I said, grinning at her.

"Oh, there's Mrs. Ambrose," Mom said. "I need to talk to her about Grad Night. Do you mind?"

"Go ahead," I said. "I'll see you backstage."

It was over. It was now or never to talk to Dev. I caught up with him outside the dressing room. He was leaning against the wall, talking to his parents and Monet. He was still in costume, although he'd loosened the tie and slung the suit jacket over his shoulder.

"Sophie, there you are," Monet said. She was holding a bouquet of daisies tied with a yellow gingham ribbon. Scott stood on her other side.

"Nice flowers," I said. I remembered I hadn't thanked Dev yet for my orchids, but I didn't want to say anything in front of his parents. Mr. Lucero liked to tease.

"Sophie, you were marvelous," Mr. Lucero said. "But I'm sorry you had to kiss my son. I hope the experience wasn't too terrible." His dimples flashed when he smiled.

He bore a remarkable resemblance to Dev. Dev and Monet got their red hair from him.

"Thank you," I replied. "It wasn't too terrible—acting opposite Dev."

"I hope he behaved himself," his mother interjected.

"Of course," I said. Dev seemed to be enthralled with an imaginary spot right over my shoulder.

We chatted for a few minutes, but his parents showed no signs of leaving.

Finally, in desperation, I said, "Dev, can I talk to you for a minute?"

He didn't move. I was definitely getting mixed signals from him.

"Son, when a beautiful woman asks you to talk to her, you go talk to her," his father said. He gave him a gentle shove in my general direction. "Your mother and I will see you later."

Monet said, "Oh, there's Vanessa. I need to talk to her about . . . something. C'mon, Scott." She winked at me before she grabbed Scott's arm and led him away.

Dev looked at me but didn't say anything.

"Thank you for the orchids," I said. "They're beautiful."

"You're welcome."

This had to be the most awkward conversation in the history of awkward conversations.

"Dev, about the costume closet," I said.

"You don't have to say anything," he said. "I know you're back with Connor."

"I'm not back with Connor," I said.

My life had been fraught with miscommunication lately. It was time to clear the air.

"Dev," I said, "I care about you, but—"

He said, "Sophie, it's okay. I saw you two together. You were happy. You don't have to sugarcoat it."

He left before I could say anything else. How could a smart guy get things so backward? And how could he possibly miss that Connor and Angie were holding hands as they passed us?

I couldn't figure it out, unless Dev was obviously not interested and was using Connor as an excuse. Anyone with a brain in his head could see that Connor and I weren't together, would never be together again, and, in fact, were much better off as friends than we ever were as boyfriend and girlfriend.

# Chapter 26

It was our last performance. I don't know if it was nostalgia or boy trouble, but I was feeling melancholy as I donned my costume for the last time.

During the play, Angie didn't stumble over any lines and there were only a few minor glitches (during the wedding scene, a piece of scenery almost toppled, but Dev had the foresight to grab it and pretend to casually lean against the faux wall until curtain).

There was no use in crying. Dev was obviously not interested in me. I vowed to give up guys permanently and devote myself to good works. Or something.

"Did you talk to him?" Monet asked.

"Your brother is insane," I said. "I talked to him, but I'm not sure he heard me. It was like we were speaking two different languages."

"He'll come around, Sophie," she said. "It's obvious he likes you."

It wasn't obvious to me. "I'll take your word for it."

I was still in costume, although I'd wiped the heavy stage paint from my face. The stuff made you break out if you left it on too long.

I helped Monet and Vanessa set up the snacks and punch for the parents.

There was even a real wedding cake that towered next to the punch bowl. I nabbed a Fig Newton and glanced around. I was pretending to ignore Dev, but unfortunately, he hadn't noticed.

"Why don't you go feed your hubby a slice of wedding cake?" Vanessa teased.

I blushed. "Cut it out."

Dev was heading to the snack table. He reached over and nabbed a cookie. He never looked my way once.

Olivia was standing a few feet away, probably just waiting to pounce. "I knew there was something between them," I overheard her say. "I saw . . ." I tuned her out. I'd heard enough gossip lately.

Evidently, so had Dev, because he abruptly turned away.

"This is our cast party?" Monet asked.

"Of course not," Vanessa snorted. "This," she waved at the innocent-looking snacks, "is for the parents' benefit. The real cast party starts later."

"For a minute, I thought you'd lost your mind," she

replied. "We're still all going to Wicked Jack's for dinner, right?"

She nodded. "And then to Haley's. Her parents said we could use the guesthouse, but not to step foot in the main house."

Haley's parents were loaded. Their guesthouse was bigger than my entire house. The thought of smiling and laughing and pretending to have fun made me tired. I just wanted to go home and sleep for about a week. And when I woke up, I wanted to eat a pint of Ben & Jerry's.

But I had obligations. I had already told Monet that we'd hang out at the cast party, and for once, I was going to keep a promise to her.

"I dropped off the snacks there earlier," I said. "But make sure that if Jason Brady shows up, someone frisks him for a flask."

"That guy should come with a warning label," Vanessa replied, "after what he tried with you."

"I don't think he'll be trying that again," I said. "I heard he tried to get grabby with Kaley Michaels and her brother practically tore him apart."

"Jason's not too bright, is he?" Vanessa replied. Kurt Michaels was an all-star linebacker with a notoriously short temper.

I chuckled. "Not very."

Dev was no longer in the room. I knew because my heart had stopped thrumming.

I smiled when I saw that Connor had given Angie a huge bouquet of roses. So predictable. I cherished my orchids, which were more exotic.

"I forgot to hang up my costume," I said. I gave Monet a rueful glance.

"We'll wait for you," she said. "Make sure to put it in the right place."

"I will," I said, summoning a smile. I didn't really feel like going to the party, but I would make an appearance. "Go on without me, but save me a seat."

I draped the costume over my arm and headed to the closet. I hung the dress up very carefully and in plain view.

The door opened and then I heard Dev clear his throat, but I didn't turn around. "Monet told me I might find you here."

"I'm supposed to meet her at the party."

"She told me to tell you it was okay," he said. "She said to tell you she'll hang out with you on Sunday instead."

"Instead of what?" I was confused.

"I—you know, I had the biggest crush on you in middle school." He looked down at his hands.

"You had a weird way of showing it."

He grinned. "I know," he said. "I tortured you unmercifully. But I had it bad."

"And now?" I couldn't look at him. I didn't want him to see the hope in my eyes.

He moved closer. "Now it's even worse."

"Why didn't you say anything? I just stood there," I said.

"I don't know," he confessed. "It was stupid. I thought you were giving me the brush-off. I wanted more than anything to —"

"To what?"

"To do this," he said. And then he kissed me.

Even though I was still mad at him, I kissed him back. What can I say? He was a great kisser.

A long time later, I remembered that we hadn't really settled anything between us. I wasn't up for another long session in the costume closet if, afterward, it meant weeks of Dev not speaking to me.

"Dev, we need to talk," I said. "I wasn't the one —"

"I know," he said. "I heard Olivia talking about it earlier. You didn't spread the rumor about us. I was an ass to think you'd do something like that."

I thought about letting it go, but I was the new, improved Sophie. New leaf and all that.

"I might have done something like that," I said sheepishly. "If I'd thought of it."

There was no sense in pretending to be someone I wasn't. Not with Dev or anyone else. He had to like me for me, not for who he wanted me to be.

His face darkened for a moment, but then he laughed. "True."

"But that was the old me," I continued. "I've changed. Or at least I'm trying to change."

"You're perfect just the way you are," he said huskily.

"No, I'm not," I said. "But I'm glad you think I am."

We engaged in several minutes of silent communication, but then I had a thought and put my hand to his chest.

"What does this mean, Dev? I'm not going to be your closet girlfriend, someone you can just kiss and leave whenever you feel like it."

He smiled slyly. "Why would I want you as a closet girlfriend when I can have the real thing?"

I was speechless. Were we finally getting our act together?

He looked alarmed. "You're not saying anything. Sophie, I know I made some mistakes, but I really like you. Can you forgive me?"

I kissed him into silence, which I hoped answered his question.

"We're going to be late for the party," I murmured.

"Do you really want to go?" he said.

"No," I said. I sighed. "But I promised Vanessa and Monet that I'd help. And I can't let Monet down. Especially since she's given me permission to date her gorgeous older brother."

He matched my sigh with one of his own. "Just a few more minutes," he said against my lips.

"A few more minutes," I agreed.

Somehow, we'd ended up on the floor again. "This," I said, "is becoming a habit."

"A very good habit," Dev said.

We resumed kissing, but a minute later, I heard the sound of a door opening.

"Not again," I groaned.

"What is it?" he said, but his hands were stroking my back, which made it hard for me to think.

"I have a very bad feeling that we have company."

We sat up and both looked toward the door. I met Olivia Kaplan's eyes.

"You guys," Olivia said, after a long moment where she stood there with her mouth agape, "you're going to miss it. Everyone's leaving for the party."

"Have fun," Dev said. "We'll get there eventually. But first I want to kiss my girlfriend." He slammed the door in her face.

"Now, where were we?" he asked.

"Hmm, I've forgotten," I teased.

"I know," he said. "Kiss me, Sophie."

And I did.

*KENNEDY HIGH SENTINEL*

*"The Taming of the Shrew"*

*This somewhat flat production of one of Shakespeare's plays was buoyed by fine performances by Dev Lucero, the luscious Sophie Donnelly, and surprisingly, even Connor Davis. Angie Vogel provided a beautiful but somewhat listless performance of the fiery Katharina. Highlights included Ms. Donnelly's subtle and graceful Bianca and Dev Lucero's passionate Lucentio. This reporter adored how the play ended with a riotous wedding banquet. And it didn't hurt that they served actual wedding cake at the closing-night cast reception.*

All's fair in love and billiards ...

For a sneak peek at another fun, romantic novel from Marlene Perez, turn the page!

From

# Love in the Corner Pocket

***by Marlene Perez***

I was just a girl in a pair of low riders who might give them a glimpse of my thong when I bent over to take a shot. Or that's what guys thought when they first played pool with me. They asked me for a game so they could stare at my ass. Guys don't *seriously* think that a mere girl can beat them at pool.

A game of pool is full of deceit. Otherwise, no one would put their money on the table, would they? I mean, if a guy knows from the beginning that I'm going to run the table, why would he play?

Since my dad left, I've had a no-guy rule. It helped me focus on the game. I hadn't even indulged in a random hookup, at least, not until Alex.

The first time I saw him was at Gino's, on a hot Friday afternoon. It was late October, well after school started.

Gino's was a restaurant on Pacific Coast Highway.

Out of the big bay window, if you craned your neck, you could see both the sunbathers and the surfers paddling out to catch the waves.

It was a dive, but we hung out there a lot. Gino never minded if we came in straight from the beach, tracking sand and dripping water everywhere. Gino's also had the best food in town. The best pool tables, too.

I was supposed to meet my best friend, Bridget, and some of our friends, but I was early, so I played cutthroat with a couple of college boys. I called the eight ball and sank it, putting the boys out of their misery. They left a few minutes later, looking like two scolded puppies.

I looked around again for Bridget and that's when I saw him. He walked in and went straight for the pool tournament sign-up sheet. I planned to win that tournament, which had a two-thousand-dollar cash prize, so at first I was just sizing up the competition.

He saw me watching him and smiled. That's all it took. The rest of the package, his sparkling gray eyes, his curly black hair, his broad shoulders, that was all icing. My brain refused to listen to what my body was saying.

When he reached up and took a cue from the rack on the wall, I held my breath. Gino was going to go ballistic. The guy in the T-shirt must not have seen the sign, the one that promised pain and suffering to anyone who touched those cues.

Gino only let a few people keep their cues on that wall and nobody else was allowed to touch them. I didn't have a cue hanging on that rack, and Gino's was my second home. Gino always said, "Be patient, your time will come."

I jumped when Gino, who was sitting at this stool at the bar, let out a great roar and came rumbling over. I thought he was going to pulverize the guy, but instead he wrapped him in a great big bear hug.

"Alex, when did you get back in town?" Gino said.

*Alex, his name was Alex.*

Gino steered him in the direction of the kitchen. "Wait until Rose sees you."

Maybe Gino felt my eyes boring into his back, because he stopped and turned around. He couldn't possibly miss me, since I was standing there with my mouth open. I'm pretty sure I looked as intelligent as a guppy.

"Chloe, I want you to meet my nephew," he hollered.

Gino practically dragged the guy over to meet me. I was worried that he would think I was a troll or something. I frantically tried to remember the last time I'd washed my hair. This morning. Fantastic. I was safe from greasy hair.

Alex snagged a mint from the big jar of peppermints on the counter. I grinned. Then he touched my hand and I swear a sizzle started in my blood. "I'm Alex Harris," he said.

"You look familiar," I said.

"Alex is an aspiring actor," Gino said. "Maybe you saw him in a commercial." He said it in the same tone he'd used to describe someone who'd skipped out on a bar tab or cheated at pool. Uncle Gino clearly wasn't a fan of his nephew's chosen profession.

Alex held my hand a second longer than strictly necessary. Then I noticed Gino grinning like a fiend and immediately dropped his hand. We stood there, smiling at each other.

"Chloe, there you are," a voice said.

Three minutes into our relationship and Alex already had to take the acid test. Bridget.

My best friend was a golden girl. She glowed from the sun, her blonde beauty dazzling everyone within view.

We first met at the beach when we were about three. We both wanted the same sand shovel. We were locked in combat when our moms came and pried us apart.

"That's *my* shovel," Bridget said. "Give it to me and I'll be your friend." She smiled the sweetest smile, and I remember thinking that she was the most beautiful girl I'd ever seen.

I let go of the shovel and she took possession of it

with a happy sigh. I immediately burst into tears and hid behind my mom.

Bridget waddled over and handed me the shovel. She put her arm around me. "Don't cry!"

But I only cried harder.

"Here, you take it. I'm sorry," she said, her dimples dancing.

But I didn't want the toy anymore. I just wanted Bridget to be my friend.

So when she came over with that same look on her face, I knew that Alex was something she wanted.

Bridget was more than a gorgeous blonde; she had that indefinable *something.* She was so far out of my league, I was barely on the same planet.

Alex said a polite hello and then resumed eye contact with me. He didn't seem to notice that the quintessential California girl was standing in front of him.

"So, Chloe," she said, not taking her eyes from Alex, "Theo's saving you a place at the table."

I stared at the floor. I remembered that the old Chloe, the one who believed in true love, was gone. It was time to make a swift exit and leave the playing field to Bridget.

"I gotta go," I muttered. "Nice to meet you." And then I practically ran. I didn't hear whatever Alex called after me.

But I heard Bridget's giggle and his low rumble of laughter in reply.

*Airhead*

*Being Nikki*

By **Meg Cabot**

*Suite Scarlett*

By **Maureen Johnson**

*Sea Change*

*The Year My Sister Got Lucky*

*South Beach*

*French Kiss*

*Hollywood Hills*

By **Aimee Friedman**

*And Then Everything Unraveled*

By **Jennifer Sturman**

*The Heartbreakers*

*The Crushes*

By **Pamela Wells**

*This Book Isn't Fat, It's Fabulous*

By **Nina Beck**

*Wherever Nina Lies*

By **Lynn Weingarten**

*Summer Girls*

*Summer Boys*

*Next Summer*

*After Summer*

*Last Summer*

By **Hailey Abbott**

**In or Out**

By Claudia Gabel

*In or Out*

*Loves Me, Loves Me Not*

*Sweet and Vicious*

*Friends Close, Enemies Closer*

**Hotlanta**
By Denene Millner
and Mitzi Miller

*Hotlanta*

*If Only You Knew*

*What Goes Around*

*Love in the Corner Pocket*

*The Comeback*

By **Marlene Perez**

*Pool Boys*

*Meet Me at the Boardwalk*

By **Erin Haft**

*Popular Vote*

By **Micol Ostow**

*Top 8*

By **Katie Finn**

*Kissing Booth*

By **Lexie Hill**

*Kissing Snowflakes*

By **Abby Sher**

**Once Upon a Prom**
By Jeanine Le Ny

*Dream*

*Dress*

*Date*

**Making a Splash**
By Jade Parker

*Robyn*

*Caitlin*

*Whitney*

*Secret Santa*

*Be Mine*

By **Sabrina James**

*21 Proms*

Edited by **Daniel Ehrenhaft**
and **David Levithan**

Point
www.thisispoint.com